"A good book can take us to an exotic locale, flood us with emotions or remind us of that special summer that awakened adulthood. A very good book can do all of these vividly, realistically, seamlessly. Indira Ganesan's *Inheritance* is such a book."

—Heidi Johnson-Wright, *Columbus Dispatch*

"*Inheritance* possesses . . . delicate grace, as well as a wisdom that is at once childlike and wry."

—Chitra B. Divakaruni, *San Francisco Chronicle*

"[Ganesan] writes a young girl's heart and mind with a true and gentle hand. The sentences in this book are languorous; they stretch like waking cats or preen like proud parrots." —Marc Munroe Dion, *Kansas City Star*

"A lithe and sinuous storyteller. . . . Ganesan, like Arundhati Roy and Chitra Divakaruni, is part of a glorious flowering of contemporary Indian literature."

—Donna Seaman, *Booklist*

"Ganesan steeps us in her world with imagery that is both sensual and precise." —*Swing*

"What makes this novel quite remarkable is its young author's writing skill. . . . The results are characters who feel real to the reader." —*Islands*

"Graceful, economical, and charming."
—Geeta Sharma-Jensen, *Milwaukee Journal*

"Lush and stylish . . . well worth reading."
—Beth E. Andersen, *Library Journal*

"A veritable naturalistic hymn to India."
—*Publishers Weekly*

INHERITANCE

ALSO BY INDIRA GANESAN

The Journey

INHERITANCE

Indira Ganesan

Beacon Press   Boston

Beacon Press
25 Beacon Street
Boston, Massachusetts 02108-2892
www.beacon.org

Beacon Press books are published under the auspices of
the Unitarian Universalist Association of Congregations

First published by Beacon Press in 1999
Printed in the United States of America

Portions of this book were originally published in different form in the
following: *Dissident Song*, *Printed Matter*, *Poughkeepsie Review*, and *Shankpainter*

07 06 05 04 03 02 01 00   8 7 6 5 4 3 2 1

This book is printed on recycled acid-free paper that contains at least 20
percent postconsumer waste and meets the uncoated paper ANSI/NISO
specifications for permanence as revised in 1992.

Library of Congress Cataloging-in-Publication Data
Ganesan, Indira
Inheritance / Indira Ganesan
    p.   cm.
ISBN 0-8070-6227-8
1. Racially mixed children—-India—Fiction.
2. India—Fiction. I. Title
[PS3557.A495I54   1999]
813'.54—dc21   99-36174

In memory of my grandmother

INHERITANCE

One

My mother awoke in the holy hour before dawn, rumple-eyed and irritable. From the branches of the coral jasmine tree, a night-flowering wonder, small orange-centered blossoms fell to the ground in slow rhythms outside her window. She let a comb creep through her hair, with her fingertips touched sandalwood oil to her throat, between her breasts, her eyes closed in dreams. Perhaps she thought of marrying again. My mother wore a sari of pale yellow, and I imagined she felt she could write a novel then and there. Didn't she have forty-six years of life to tell?

But in came my grandmother, scattering my mother's thoughts away, shuffling on feet that had turned as hard as stone. Trumpeting words like an elephant, she asked my mother, "Have you brushed your teeth yet? Do you

want your coffee now?" My mother, caught in her
dreams, caught with her hand on her breast, nodded
yes. The house was awake. The maids began to wash
the dishes from the night before, and the cook yelled at
them while cutting vegetables. The orange vendors and
tomato sellers were already at the doorstep, calling out
their wares. In the midst of this morning chaos, it was
my mother who was labeled the maddest. She was the
strange one, the daughter gone wrong, the bad woman
who refused to go to temple, who needed her own
mother to fetch her morning coffee, who would not wear
widow-white. "Why should I wear white if I still have
fifty years more of my life to live?" she had asked when
her first husband died, refusing to look at my grandmother's face.

I imagined my mother in the mornings like this,
imagined her thoughts, her longings. She did not speak
to me. When I was six, and arrived at my grandmother's
house on the island of Pi, dusty and yet presentable after
a sultry train and boat journey from India, only my
grandmother and Great-uncle Raj were at the table
set for the midday meal. Even before I saw her bold-
patterned sari and unbound hair, I knew my mother was
watching me, suspicious, from a corner. For days we
edged past each other. She spoke no words to me.

When I turned fifteen, I came to my grandmother's
house for a long stay, this time to rest, to get over a drag-
ging spell of bronchitis. I had been given four months
leave from my pre-university. My life was filled with so

much illness that I had become a kind of heroine for my younger cousins. ("This is Sonil," they told their friends. "She gets a lot of diseases.") There were hardly two days apart when I was not sick. It was when the huskiness in my voice was lifting, and my chest no longer ached as if a tiger were walking about inside, that my grandmother suggested I spend the summer months at her home, away from the infected cities.

"The island air is so good—she'll recover well," wrote my grandmother to my guardian aunts in Madras.

"And Lakshmi, what about Lakshmi? Has she recovered as well?" whispered my aunts on the phone.

Lakshmi: that name had been whispered, lingered over in soft tones in my undetected presence for years. My mother, Lakshmi, who hadn't seen me in nine years. Only from the merest shreds of conversation had I gathered bits of my mother's story. They would not tell me the whole truth, so I became an eavesdropper, not knowing they shielded me from whatever harm could be imparted in words. It would be unthinkable, they said, to live with my mother. Only bad would come of it, they thought. What are they afraid of? Would she spit at me, scream at me, shake me as enraged madwomen do in the movies? Or was it simply the association they feared, that her strange ways would rub off on me, the way certain flowers left gold dust on my fingers? But despite the protests, my grandmother, who can wear a face as strong as any god's, had her way.

So I went to Pi, to spend a summer full of change

and wonder. It was a summer of attuned perceptions, a turnover, a prelude to adulthood; even now, I have not fully recovered from it. It was a summer of awakening. My grandmother's house was different from my home in Madras. Here, I could walk under the mango trees in a place that lacked only a waterfall to make it a kind of paradise. In the mornings, tiny parrots, blazes of red and green, rushed into the skies that were brighter than any in Madras. The trees were full of monkeys, bright fruit stuffed into their mouths. I could make a telescope out of my hands and see their glittery old-man eyes.

Since she wouldn't speak to me, I spied on my mother, wanting to learn the facts, the truths to tie a kind of monkey-knot to her, a knot that could not be undone. I wanted to know about the circumstances before and after my birth. They had said my arrival was not graceful.

They wouldn't let my mother in the kitchen, I observed, to ward off the evil that must surround her, to keep it away from the most holy place in the house. She would take her coffee outside to the brick steps near the pots of roses. She would snap off a deep red bud to adorn herself, having no patience to wait for the lame girl who sold stringed jasmine wound with sage to wear in one's hair. My mother, from her perch, and I, from mine, kept abreast of the flirtations between the cook's daughter and the driver, noting the way he casually brushed by the daughter's perfumed arms before my great-uncle rushed out for his morning drive. They didn't worry about my mother's gaze, so inconsequential was she.

My mother was infuriating. She refused to eat with the rest of us, making Grandmother set an extra plate for her after we'd eaten, before she, my grandmother, could eat. My grandmother insisted on serving all of us, Mother included, before she herself ate. This I did not think was nice of my mother, to delay my grandmother's dinner. But maybe my grandmother enjoyed the conversation with my mother, for the two of them often spoke together for two hours, one for my mother's dining, one for my grandmother's. Their voices were only murmurs, hard for me to hear.

Maybe my mother ran away from me because there was a gene in our family that caused people to run and hide. Our family was shy, excepting my mother, and even she might be shy, for wouldn't that have caused her to flee from me, her third daughter? For she did run away, run away from the American, my father, and leave me to my aunts.

My mother had three daughters. Her first she presented to a husband who wanted a son; she tried to fix things by choosing a name that could pass for masculine: Ramani. After her husband died, taking his secrets to the fire, several trendy college girls began to invite my mother, lovely at twenty-one, to their lawn parties. At one party, a rich boy, coolly dressed after the fashion dictated by his affected English accent, a filmmaker's son, promised to marry my mother. Whether she believed him or not, surely she was seduced by his voice, which ran like warm champagne. She named his child after Savitri, the most dutiful of wives in Hindu legend, a woman whose footsteps followed her husband's even after his death. My mother didn't trail after the filmmaker's boy, though. She met an American expatriate, a photographer who came to Pi to capture on film the faces of wise seers and shy, mysterious women. The village women say she asked him to sleep with her, and he accepted, and she gave birth to me.

They named me Sonil, a name with no definite roots. When I was younger, I used to make up stories regarding my father's death and my mother's grief, but they brought me nowhere. My parents remained as distant as any in a thousand tales from folklore. Why did she want a third daughter? What caused her need to be full of another baby? Why did she send him away? Perhaps my mother had always wanted to raise a troop of strong highway-bandit queens by herself, and perhaps she was prevented. She would have been a good robber rani herself, a brave woman with a fearless stance. She stood straight under the scrutinizing eyes of neighbors whose mouths never closed. She watched the brightly saried servant girls who gossiped loudly at the gate, catching the hush of their voices when they spoke of her. She was the only woman who didn't turn away in disgust when Ramachandran, the senile gatekeeper, hunched with age, lifted up his dhoti to relieve himself under the banyan trees in the opposite lot.

They must have told her she was different, to give her that boldness. Some chanting woman in an orange sari and with a shaven head must have gripped her hand and told her she had the fingers of an artist. Some troupe of fanatics leading a cow wearing streamers and bells, shaking with an intensity that only the most devout or near insane have, must have told her she was not meant for a peaceful widowhood. They must have told her it was fine to wear bangles and anklets, emboldened her to conceive two more children after her first, freed her to think of marrying again in her forty-seventh year. But who would marry a madwoman? If she advertised in the marital columns, only self-proclaimed free-thinking widowers would answer her ad, and who knew how crazy they were? No one would answer from Madhupur, or from the other towns nearby. On the island of Pi, reputations traveled.

Lunchtime, and Great-uncle Raj was trying to teach me Italian. He was my grandmother's eldest brother, a man whose eccentricity almost surpassed my mother's. Long ago, my great-uncle had a job with a company that sent him overseas. For two months, he traveled in Europe, pretending not to be a tourist. When the company asked for his return, he refused and was fired. He stayed on abroad, coming home only for funerals. But one year, seven of our relatives died, and he ran out of money. So he made his home at my grandmother's, but he spoke of his travels constantly. He knew dozens of languages and spent long hours at the USIS library, reading foreign dailies. Once I saw him there with stacks of thin-sheeted papers in front of him, wearing the smile of the truly indulged. Now he insisted on coaxing Italian stresses from my tongue, finding my progress slow. My grandmother interrupted the lesson.

"How are you feeling? Are you well? Do you have a temperature?" she asked.

A dozen times a day, she questioned me about my health. She made up careful menus of non-fried foods for me and sent back reports to Madras. (Vasanti, the cook, felt sorry for me and sometimes sneaked outlawed savories and buttery pooris to my plate.) Great-uncle, annoyed at the disturbance to his lesson, rose from the table, leaving me with unlearned verbs. My grandmother brushed crumbs from the table.

"Don't believe his nonsense, Sonil-ma," she said. "He doesn't know a word of Italian."

Vasanti was going into town for groceries, a plastic bag from Paris, a relic from my great-uncle, in her hand. She met my mother on her way to hang her wet saris, a tangle of color, on the terraced roof.

"Do you want anything from the shops?" asked Vasanti.

"A jar of Pond's—a large one," replied my mother.

"And something for your daughter?" asked Vasanti who thought she was being diplomatic. "Should I buy her something?"

My mother pretended not to hear. Sometimes I wanted to scream, to shout out loud, I AM YOUR DAUGHTER, TALK TO ME! I wanted to force her to regard me, to stop pretending I didn't exist, to stop denying my part in her life. I could accept her madness, but not her hatred. If all her acts could be explained away by her madness, then I was safe, because she was not responsible for her actions. To ask why she didn't want to raise me herself, to wonder why she continued to live at my grandmother's house then became moot. Vasanti left by the back door, and my mother climbed the outer stairs. The milkman had come at dawn to deliver our milk. I thought of his bicycle clattering away on the pavement and began to dream of going away, of leaving everyone behind. I wanted to travel fast.

Feeling the pull of the afternoon, my grandmother lay down on the couch to read the mail. There was a letter from my sister Ramani full of house-talk and news of her children. Both of my sisters were pregnant again and neither planned to invite our mother to her baby's first birthday celebration. They liked her even less than I did. I pressed my grandmother's feet and told her my dreams.

Because I had nothing else to do but read while I was sick, I pulled first marks in all the school exams. In the room I shared with two cousins in Madras, I'd tacked up a picture of an American college from a catalogue a teacher had once given me. If I continued to do well, and if I took a qualifying exam in Delhi, I told myself I could go to Radcliffe.

"What is that place?" asked my grandmother.

"Do you know *Love Story*? *Love Story* took place there," I said.

My grandmother in her wisdom glasses looked at the wall a long time before replying.

"I don't think I approve of that sort of life, Sonil," she said.

The sun had calmed for a moment, but it would be back, fierce as ever. The village herders brought back the indifferent cows from pasture. Their thin bodies passed like ghosts behind the gate. The sweets seller made his late rounds while the iron man clattered his cart down the street. My grandmother was in the back garden, watering the plants. I rocked myself on the veranda swing, sucking experimentally on the cigarette butts my great-uncle had left behind. While I tried to compose a letter to my aunts, I could pick out from the street the voice of the man who sold pinwheels and silver ribbons to children.

Two of my aunts raised me, both sisters of my

mother's, Aunt Leila and Aunt Shalani. Aunt Leila was thin and Aunt Shalani even thinner. They were warm-hearted, the two of them, indulgent with their riches. Their husbands, Uncle Petrov and Uncle Dan, were in Abu Dhabi, oil investors by night, engineers by day. They were Russian and Irish; my mother wasn't the only one in her family to look outside the island or India for marriage. Uncle Petrov had grown up in North India and met Aunt Leila at a plant bazaar, an Indo-Russo event of cultural exchange. Uncle Dan had been schooled in Scotland and met Aunt Shalani at the home of his parents, who lived in Mysore. They married and had no children, while Aunt Leila had four. The two uncles decided to try their luck in the Middle East when I was ten and set off from India. They stayed overseas and sent home money. If my aunts missed their husbands, they didn't show it, having decided to merge their two households and visit Abu Dhabi twice a year. Twice a year, the uncles visited, so their marriages were seasonally conjugal, an arrangement that suited all. My favorite cousin, Jani, was looked after by my grandfather's sister (on my mother's side) in Delhi, but she visited us as well.

"So you smoke."

It was my mother. She seated herself on the swing, tucking her legs under her sari. I could smell a mixture of perfume and hard-milled soap from her hands. The first button on her blouse was undone, exposing flesh I was carefully trying not to look at. Casually, I offered her a butt, but she grasped my other hand instead.

"Look," she said, uncurling my fingers. She traced the lines around my thumb, the arch of my palm. "This is the heart line, this is the psychic cross, this is the mount of Venus," she said, running her fingers lightly across the marks on my palm. She placed her hand next to mine, stretching it open like a flower. "They're alike," she said. "We could be twins."

I was too astonished to say anything. She dropped my hand and began to walk back to the roof, leaving my hands hard fists, her face broken with laughter.

"No, I won't be like you!" I shouted.

I would not live on the edge of things as she did, I thought, a strange, bizarre, unnatural creature, a scornful observer. I resolved to dress in sober clothes, to wear my hair tight behind my ears, and to grow old and dignified in spite of my mother.

The sun was dazzling, touching everything with light. The roses were so bright, they seemed to tremble with color, and, dully, I could make out the sound of the monkeys which never shut up. A clatter of pebbles sounded from the roof. Looking up, I saw my mother standing straight as a bony tree against that vivid sky. With her mocking eyes upon me, she began to dance with broad steps, waving a sun-dried sari around her head. I was arrested by the sight.

Two

I was sunburnt by my mother. She was the incandescent light in my life, illuminating my days with an anger that tempted me to kick at rocks and stones. If I saw her face, my teeth ached with rage. Often she was inactive, a model of repose, an Indian odalisque, luxuriously lazy. Unlike my grandmother, who gardened incessantly, or even my great-uncle, who shaped pieces of wood to build fantastic toy cities, my mother did nothing. She lay on a chair, drying her hair, occasionally smoothing sunscreen onto her face and hands. Never did she gaze at me with curiosity as I did at her. I schemed to get her attention.

I wanted to pull her hair, tug at her ears as babies did, I wanted to cry for milk. At night, she became a darkened moon, and I was left cold. Sometimes the loneliness was so great I crept into my grandmother's bed where she held me warmly. I buried my face in my grand-mother's sari and stared at the night through the mosquito netting. I'd awaken cranky.

Once, while my mother slept at noon in the front room, I snuck into her bedroom. Her bed was swathed under netting, a silk coverlet stretched tight across its frame. Her pillows were hard, filled with feathers tightly packed, her sheets cool. Her dresser held boxes of lacquer and wood, containing jewelry. I found a silver ring with a peace sign on it, a hippie ornament, and wondered if my father had given it to her. I searched the drawers for letters but found none. Her underwear was plain, her blouses neatly stacked. I felt a little ill snooping through her clothes, so I shut the drawers. A few sticks of incense were stuck into a burner, and a small painting of a nature view was propped in a corner. It was mostly green and yellow, fields seen through a window. In the distance, mountains. Did she dream over this picture, long to flee through the grass, across the hill? Who painted it for her? No signature. I turned to her vanity, a low table topped by an ancient, heavy mirror. Her emollients were arranged in bottles and jars: face cream, neck cream, eye cream. Softeners for the hands. Cucumber water for cooling down. Rose essence for fragrance. A nearly empty bottle of foreign perfume. For whom did she beautify herself? Whom did she meet in secret on those occasions when she left the house? Whose arms held her?

I looked into her mirror, seeing what features I had from her. Eyes perhaps, a bit of the nose. But her chin was sharp where mine was soft. My cheeks were still full, baby cheeks, the kind people like to pinch and kiss. Where my mother was beauty, I was ugly, a changeling child, a half-breed, a mistake. Feeling destructive, I unscrewed her perfume bottle, so the perfume would vanish into the heat. I wanted to pierce a hole into her, to drain her smugness, her indifference. I wanted to go to sleep and awaken to discover a loving mother in her place, one who tied ribbons in my hair, who swept me into her arms. I wanted to be praised, boasted of, scolded a little. But I was stuck with a mother who paid more attention to her body than to her daughters.

My sisters had a different attitude. But they were older than I, and had their own families to think of. They pretended my mother didn't exist, content to bask in the glow of my aunts or cousins, their husbands and children. They did not miss my mother, they had erased her from their lives. She was an embarrassment, a thought flicked away. But she consumed me. I felt I was only half, that she took my soul somehow, that she kept it from me. My identity was lost, and I did not know who I was. She named me Sonil but gave me nothing else.

Perhaps something had happened to her, perhaps something so dreadful that her heart had iced overnight. Perhaps a catastrophe such as I could not comprehend had stolen her kindness or her concern and replaced it with bitterness. My mother's mystery—I would find its secret. I would plumb her history, worm out the details, free her past to learn what had happened to her. My Aunt Shalani had a friend whose daughter was struck by a car. It left her with a personality disorder. Perhaps my mother mistakenly wandered into a minefield and set off an old explosive, but there had not been a war on Pi for a hundred years. Even the Freedom Movement was on paper—no salt marches, no fasts, no brother killing. Gandhi had no need to visit the island, for it didn't need him; like a small tug following a ship, it relied on the back waves to lift it into a new era; it expended no energy of its own. Once, a militant group from Sri Lanka had landed on these shores to stir up funds and sympathy, but the apathy with which they met led the militants to retreat. There is a saying: For the future, invest in Indian computers; to write with a quill, come to Pi.

But what accident had my mother met with, to leave her so cruel and unfulfilled a woman? What ate her stomach, to leave it so lean and hard? I would have to work hard to find her truth.

They say she tried to take her life once. She was in a strange city, somewhere in the north, and she tried to fling herself from a window. She carried stones in her hands to weigh herself down, thinking perhaps that she might fly up instead. But as she placed her foot on the air, to test its nothingness, someone came into the room and screamed. It could have gone either way; my mother could have continued her action and hurtled to the ground. And with her stones, she would have fallen heavily onto the pavement. But the scream—I think it was a maidservant's—brought her to her senses, and, embarrassed, she withdrew her suicidal foot. The maidservant would not be bribed, however, and my mother returned home under the supervision of some family elders. I heard the story by chance, listening to servants' talk, being where I shouldn't have been.

Her despair must have been great, her marriage unhappy. This was when she had only two children. But the scream had saved her and, as a consequence, me. I think she tried to slash her wrists later. I know one of our relatives did, and I have always thought it was my mother. Who else could be so selfish? I did not care much to cast my mother as a great tragedienne. Thinking of my grandmother only made me think my mother was selfish. Selfish more than cowardly. Wanting her way. Marrying whomever she pleased, seeing however many men she pleased. For my mother was wanton with her affections and gave herself freely to a variety of lovers. I don't think she gave her heart away to my father, for she still toyed with many. Like a cat with a ball of yarn, she'd play with one, then another, and then, tiring of them, slink back home to sup on milk. I believed I'd catch her licking her lips; I believed I could read her thoughts.

What proof did I have of my mother's indiscretions? I never saw the men; I might have hit them if I had. Only the whispers, the stares, the laughs, indicated her wantonness, her open desires. Her late hours, her constant slipping away from the house and returning to sleep for hours. The emollients on her dresser, the lilt of her hips as she walked. My grandmother said nothing, it was out of her hands. Perhaps she argued with my mother when I wasn't around. I sometimes saw my mother with multiple arms and multiple breasts, like the bizarre temple paintings one sees in remote villages, the kind that other children's mothers hurriedly wave their babies away from. A monster of carnal desire, a rakshasha like the one who tried to seduce Rama and Lakmana. A sister of Ravana and a would-be seductress who got her nose chopped off. Except that my mother never had her face disfigured; she always remained the victor. She disgusted me, yet I couldn't ignore her. I wanted to find out what part of her was me.

Three

Joining me that summer at my grandmother's was Jani. Despite her great spirit and flair for fashion, my cousin was afraid of the dark, timid as a mouse when it came to certain things. For example, if she wanted to go to a film, it could only be a matinee or else our great-uncle had to accompany us. Ice cream only in the afternoon and never at the night bazaars.

I used to tell her, "Look, I will protect you with the saber that once belonged to our grandfather, and before that, to a real maharajah. Its blade is dull, and most of the jewels have fallen out, but I can smash a green coconut with it." True, the sword would only make a soft dent on the coconut to expose a bit of the hairy fibers, a hint of brown husk inside, but I thought it would prove my point. "And if a robber came for us, I could protect us both," I told my cousin. But she just smiled and shook her head.

Jani had introduced me to books at an early age. We would go together to the British Consulate Library in Madras and later come home to read our prizes in the shade. The library was a stuffy place, with a trio of circulating fans massaging the air. There were always people occupying every table, students taking notes, businessmen reading the paper. The librarians would not permit anyone to sleep, but people did anyway, hidden by stacks of hardbound books.

When I first visited the library with Jani, I must have been six or so. I remember clinging to my cousin's hand and going through the doors. I wandered around the children's section, fingering the backs of fairy tales, nature tales, adventures. I was dizzy with happiness. Overcoming my awe, I began to pull out the books that interested me. By the time Jani came back for me, I held a stack of fifteen and was reaching for more. Mortified, she replaced all but the first three. "We can come back," she hissed.

By the time I was thirteen, I kept notebooks like Jani, and had acquired a library of my own, of sorts, a shelf of books bought whenever I had extra money. Jani told me that in Delhi she had a shelf full of her notebooks, thin books each tied with a different-colored ribbon. She bought a special kind of notebook, the kind without any lines, holding maybe eighty sheets of paper. She lined the inside cover with pretty patterned paper, the kind used in bookbinding, lovely marbleized patterns with a satiny finish, or dainty fields of flowers. The outside she covered with a stiffer paper and then glued a picture to that. She had pictures of a girl standing at a seashore, the inside of a church in Italy, a couple of reproductions from the Ajanta caves, an old-fashioned map with strange spelling. Inside, she wrote all sorts of things, favorite poems, lists of her favorite songs, names she particularly liked. She also made diary entries that she wouldn't permit me to see. She pressed flowers inside the pages, copied embroidery patterns and kolum designs, and sometimes sketched a nice scene or even painted a tiny watercolor. They were wondrous things, her work, and very dear to her.

Jani had visited me in Madras at my aunts' house earlier in the year before I went to my grandmother's. Aunt Leila and Aunt Shalani sent me shopping to buy some school supplies and new clothes. In July, I would be returning to P.U.C., pre-university college, called Our Lady Mary Mother of God. It was a pretty college, peopled with lots of brisk nuns in grey and white, camouflaged as doves. Some were from the French islands of Indonesia, and others, non-Catholics, were from Delhi and Madras.

I still missed my old school, my worn desk and my

blue and white uniform, my lovely pencil case with its sliding top. I had decided to buy a slimmer case, more sophisticated. It was one of the things on my shopping list. I also needed to get a steel ruler in centimeters, a compass and protractor, though God knows what for, and two or three notebooks, some pencils, and a good fountain pen that didn't trail black on my fingers. I wanted an eraser—a transparent green one from Germany that smelled like candy—and a new satchel to carry everything in. Plus some everyday clothes. Here I could be fitted for some salwar kameezes. I refused to wear half-saris. Half-saris—a long skirt and blouse, and a bit of scarf to make yourself modest—are what the girls who sat up front wore. I was tired of sitting at the front; I wanted the back row.

Jani took me shopping and told me that if I stopped squirming like a child, we could have ice cream at the tea shop. I resented being bribed, but I tried to behave myself anyway. After all, I liked ice cream. Only, the seamstress was a fool and kept recommending the wrong patterns for my salwar. Patiently I explained that I didn't want the large rose print that would make me look like a chair but the striped grey and green and the one in pale blue, batik-like. Also I begged for a pink tunic that I could wear with tight black pajamas, which Jani finally conceded to after I pointed out how much less indecent a big top over skinny pants was than the tight kameezes over the baggy salwars. Then I got six cotton underpants, which I really loved even though I had sat next to a girl who bragged about the French lace ones she and her sister wore, and—to Jani's amusement—two baby brassieres. I refused to try them on and simply chose a size, which Jani, dimpled to keep from laughing, gently replaced with ones that would fit more properly. No socks—hurrah!—but what to do for shoes? I chose a sturdy pair meant for walking, the kind I imagined zoologists wore in the field.

I took two hours to select a fountain pen. I insisted on trying them all, asking the clerk for two kinds of paper, the smooth, white, unlined kind and the blotty school blue. Finally I found one with a thickish nib that had a lovely green marbled casing. I got two bottles of ink, blue and black, and practiced my name several times until I was satisfied. It was important to have a good pen, one that wouldn't skip or suddenly go dead in the middle of a chain of notes, one that would inspire me with the confidence to write good exams. I knew a girl who had cried for an hour because her special Parker pen, which she had used only for her exams for three years in a row, finally split its nib. She was terrified that, with her luck gone, she'd fail and have to do the year over.

Satisfied with my choices, I next decided on a pencil case. Jani and I chose a simple black metal one and some brightly colored pencils from Japan. Notebooks next. Schoolgirl ones with pictures of the gods or saints on the front were to be abandoned (though I dearly loved them) for quieter designs. We took some dull geometric ones, but I would cover them with prettier paper later on. I was excited by the look of my purchases neatly wrapped in white paper and tied with twine. I loved the smell of new stationery and was very happy to sniff all the ink and the just sharpened lead of new pencils, the clean scent of fresh paper, and to listen to the gentle creak of a book binding. I would use my very best handwriting the first few days, elegantly taking notes until my regular scrawl would take over and pictures would fill the margins. How sorry I'd be when my notebooks became sullied, but how inevitable was their fall.

At the tea shop, Jani and I spoke of our plans. I wanted to become a zoologist, renowned for my work with chimpanzees or arachnids.

"Spiders!" exclaimed Jani.

"Why not? You can't be afraid of them, Jani. They're so small—and cute."

Jani shuddered, and I quickly asked her what she wanted to become.

"I don't want to become anything. I will finish my studies and perhaps work as a teacher, or as a nurse, if I take an additional two years in health science," she said. Then, smiling, she added, "I just want a quiet life, no drama, no tension, just calmness and serenity."

"I want some adventure, and I want to travel. I want to go to Africa and America," I said. Jani laughed.

"What will you find in America?"

"Maybe my father." I didn't mean to say that but the words fell out. Jani was silent.

"Perhaps you shouldn't dig around in the past," she said.

I didn't know what to say. I never spoke about her parents to Jani; I thought it would make her too sad. And Jani in turn never spoke to me much about mine. A long time ago, she had said that we were not bound by who had made us, that the only person we had to answer to was God.

The two of us plunged into our own thoughts for a while, silently spooning ice cream into our mouths. I imagined a smart life for myself, one spent in Kenya, Sri Lanka, and possibly the Amazon. I wanted something exciting, something different from my cousins and my friends who, I felt, would be confined within India. I did not want to be landlocked, and I saw my fortune beyond the sea. I knew I wanted to do something with my life, something extraordinary. When I was ten, I wrote a list of possibilities for my future, amazing things. I was going to be a deep-sea diver, a scuba explorer, a coral reef and anemone finder. I wanted to help colonize the oceans, build cities amid the mermaids, wear conch flowers in my hair, dangle sea horses from my ears. Then I thought I'd work with animals, ride around in a zebra-patterned truck, make friends among the pachyderms and newborn panthers. I wanted to live with gorillas, to live with lions. At fifteen, I still did. I wanted to be another Jane Goodall. And I wanted to meet a rock-and-roll star. My dreams were limitless.

Jani could live in India, and I would write her letters, and perhaps we'd meet once or twice a year, brimming with news, and happy with our lives. Our future was pretty bright, only Jani did not look so happy. I tried to reassure her, telling her we could always meet at our grandmother's. The island would always be ours.

"Life changes you as you become older, Sonil," said Jani. "Things that were once important don't seem so necessary. Maybe you'll understand that someday."

"The *core* of me will always remain the same. I'll always be true to my dreams. We have to be," I said.

"Dreams are funny. They're ideas, playthings, food for thought. But they don't give you sustenance."

I disagreed but didn't argue. I was firm in my beliefs.

My holidays were to begin and end in May. But my bronchitis arrived two days after Jani's visit. I stopped going to school, and after two weeks I was sent to the island. Jani would join me soon, after her college let out in April. March, April, May, June, before my second-year pre-university course started. Four months on the island, four months to recover, four months to dream. Four months with a mother whose riddle I'd solve. Four months with my grandmother whom I adored. And four months to perhaps uncover what my cousin meant by her ideas on dreams.

Four

My grandmother's house was old-fashioned, so old-fashioned that the Indus Valley civilizations probably had similar houses in 3000 B.C. Around an open courtyard with a young jasmine tree (the kind that dropped hundreds of flowers when you shook its slender trunk) and a pedestal of holy basil, nine rooms were situated. One was the kitchen, with a gas burner, a small refrigerator, and a storeroom off to the side where rice, lentils, and sweets were stored. A vat of vadumangoes was ready for frequent sampling, and another stored grown mango pickles, floating in hot oil, that is, in chili oil. My grandmother loved to make pickles, drying the mangoes picked from her trees outside in the courtyard, slicing and arranging on trays, finally soaking them in spice. Sometimes her neighbors came over to help make pa-

padum. A group of women gathered in the courtyard, busily working dough into compact circles, chattering, having fun, talking all day, then going home with an equal share of the goods.

One summer, there were no papadums. This was when my grandmother fell ill. I was ten, on holiday, on my second visit to the island.

The Mystic of Madhupur told me how to save my grandmother. She said if I were to sit in front of a lighted candle, if I made a space in my heart and concentrated, and carefully drew a mandala for seven days, I could ease my grandmother's pain.

I had gone to the Mystic in desperation one day when my grandmother could not stop trembling. At first she had trembled only at night, and the pills the doctor prescribed calmed her, but later she began to shake all the time, and complained of aches in her limbs. She had an illness of the nervous system, the doctor said, something that possessed her legs and would not allow her to rest. So she spent her days on the hard wood couch that served her as a bed. She lay on her side, swathed in a green cotton sari, a gently breathing hill in our house. My mother was away at the time and I saw little of my great-uncle.

"But I don't know how to draw a mandala," I told the Mystic. It was true—I was terrible at drawing. My trees looked like Africa balanced on a popsicle stick; my birds looked like loosened turbans.

"Mandalas can be drawn by connecting an infinite number of circles to squares," said the Mystic.

The Mystic lived on King George Street. I had never been there before, forbidden by my grandmother to come within even two blocks of it. It was in a run-down section of town, flanked by government-built housing for the poor, drab buildings made of concrete with a veneer of pee and graffiti. They were full of crying babies and harried mothers. The sidewalk was blanketed by swarms of flies that shifted only slightly as you walked through, resettling lazily. The Mystic lived at the very end of the street, near a vacant lot that served as a common dump site, a home for the homeless.

My grandmother had told me stories about the Mystic, how she could cure snakebite and spider poison, how she could heal gaping wounds and broken legs. She had been honored for her medicinal cures until the doctors in town, or maybe it was the priests, or the bureaucrats, or the mothers, someone, became scared and jealous and declared her mentally unstable, dangerous to the community. She had lived for a time on Queen Victoria Street, where many merchants lived, but they chased her to King George Street, where she continued to practice her art. She could look at your toes and tell your future.

I gave her my birthday money. She dipped a sprig of jasmine in a bowl of water and shook it over my head as she ushered me out.

"Make a different mandala every day," she repeated, refusing to say more.

Because they had seen me leave the Mystic's shack, the men who had earlier taunted me or stood in my way to demand money now left me alone. I walked unbothered to Queen Victoria Street, but hardly recognized my surroundings, so concentrated was I on my task. I decided to go to the local library to research mandalas. A man stood on the steps, his arms mere stumps, an empty can around his neck for change. After I dropped some coins in the can, he continued to look at me with huge dark eyes out of a caved-in, grizzly-chinned face. "I can't help you," I forced myself to say, "I have to help my grandmother."

Mandalas, I discovered, are also called cosmograms, and represent the entire world in a small picture. They signify the power of interrelation, of the interdependency of all things, of the separate layers to all life. I learned that the ancient Aztecs had mandalas, and so did the Greeks and the Hebrews, that mandalas could be found in the rose windows of the great cathedrals. I read that in New York City a Tibetan monk had made a mandala out of colored sands, a complex representation of many worlds with intricate designs, and had then brushed the whole thing carefully into a jar and deposited it in a river. It was an act for peace.

· · ·

The armless man was gone when I came out. I had a chance to look at the library wall. It was a popular place for impassioned writing, and I checked out the new graffiti. PROMOTE NUCLEAR DISARMAMENT, I read. ADC OUT OF OFFICE, and FREE NELSON MANDELA. Every day, for two weeks now, someone had scrawled this last message, and every day, for two weeks, someone had white-washed it away. There was nothing else interesting, so I moved on.

My grandmother had given me my first drawing lesson. She drew a large circle, then a small circle right on top of it; adding whiskers and ears, eyes and a tail, she had a cat. My grandmother's hands were large and wrinkled, ancient-looking hands that could hold an entire bird in either palm. She used to make me rice pancakes for breakfast, spreading the batter into cat shapes. I loved it when my grandmother served me food; the flavor seemed to be imparted from her hands. Now we had a cook to prepare the meals.

My grandmother had lived for three years in Malaysia and knew some words in Cantonese. It was always a marvel to me that she'd lived in a land so far away from home, where people spoke a different language and ate fish with chopsticks all day. Women rode bicycles there with their tunics billowing in the wind, my grandmother said. She had a box of black lacquer, etched with ivory dragons and flowers. I'd trace the whorls of dragon breath and wish I could see what she had seen.

For my first mandala, I chose blue and green watercolors to paint on pale violet paper. I knew that for the power to work, I'd have to draw truly, without hesitation; I couldn't sketch first. I made a box and put a circle inside it. I decided to stop there, not wanting to take chances. I left it to dry on my desk, and it seemed to me to be a flag.

My grandmother called me, and I went to press her feet. Her feet had hard, cracked calluses on the soles, from years of labor and walking. They always distressed me, for they looked painful, but she would scoff at my sentiment. "They are evidence of a good life," she'd say, but I didn't believe her. I massaged her feet with oil and then braided her hair. As if in irony, ever since her illness, her hair had been growing luxuriantly, winding down her back like a silver rope.

On the second day, I drew concentric circles in orange on yellow paper. It looked like a sun, and I liked the effect. The first mandala had curled up, so I pressed it between two books. I reminded myself to use less water. I cleaned my brushes by dipping them in an old coffee tin and squeezing out the water with my fingertips. In school, we always used dainty teacups in which the water became muddy with color too fast, and we weren't allowed to use our fingers. I had nearly failed Drawing and Painting last year. Never mind, I told my grandmother, I do well in everything else and can still go to a good college. The third day, I drew a box, and inside it I placed a diamond. Inside the diamond, I placed another box and inside that, another diamond. I finished with one more box. It looked like a lotus.

That was the day the doctor came to visit, and I painted while he examined my grandmother in the next room. Even though I was ten, he still gave me sucking candy. He smiled at me when he had finished in my grandmother's room and asked me to get the prescription filled. With my mouth full of lively peppermint, I rode my bike to the pharmacy. On the way I passed the library wall. Underneath FREE NELSON MANDELA, the whitewasher, tired and possibly fed up, had written WE ARE NOT RESPONSIBLE. I stood there awhile and realized that with a letter change, Mandela was like the word "mandala." I wondered if that was significant.

The next day, I drew a square, a diamond, a circle, another diamond, and another circle.

. . .

Mrs. Narayan from across the street called me over. She was watering her roses, which were famous all over town for their size and fragrance. She attributed the success of her gardening to a singular devotion to Laxshmi, goddess of wealth and prosperity. On her dining-room walls were beautiful life-size murals of the goddess rising from a lotus, showering gold coins from her hands.

Mrs. Narayan and my grandmother had grown up together, neighbors until the time of Mrs. Narayan's marriage. After her husband's death, Mrs. Narayan had moved back to town. It was a ritual between our two houses that she sent over two roses for us each morning, one for our family shrine, one for my hair. I disdained her gift, thinking it too old-fashioned to wear flowers in my hair. My mother was the one fond of flowers, not I. My grandmother frowned at this—young girls, she believed, had a duty to adorn themselves.

"How is your grandmother?" asked Mrs. Narayan.

"Fine," I said, looking at the ground. I will not cry, I told myself, I will not run into her arms. I stood still as she tucked a rose into my hairband.

"Pray to Laxshmi," she said. "She is our benefactress."

I wandered over to the library to see the latest development. I was not disappointed. Under the defensive WE ARE NOT RESPONSIBLE, someone had very neatly, in thick black paint, written this:

EVERYONE is responsible. It is ridiculous to excuse oneself in the face of a crime and a gross injustice. If you accept money from a thief, you participate in the robbery. By refusing to take action on acts of cruelty and prejudice, you condone the injustice. Silence is shame. Silence is the closed eye. Free one prisoner and you free yourself.

I made two more mandalas the next two days. The first one was in gold and blue and featured a box in a circle and another box and circle inside that. It looked like a television screen. The second one was better. I made a box and a circle as before, but this time I put a diamond in it, and then a box and a circle inside that. I painted it in four colors, and it seemed to be as powerful as Shiva's third eye. He is the Destroyer; he is the Creator. For the first time in a long time, I prayed to the gods to help my grandmother, to stop her pain. I read aloud to her that evening, from Dickens, but she fell asleep before I had gotten very far.

Morning, and my grandmother was still asleep. There was a large lizard on the wall, staring at me with its ugly eyes. Lizards are good, my grandmother said, they eat mosquitoes, they bring good luck. But I didn't like them; I thought they were creepy. When I was younger, I would shout for my grandmother when I'd seen one, and she would calmly catch it between the straws of a broom and shake it outdoors. I was painting a mandala that was a dark, velvety purple, the deepest color. I smiled to think that my grandmother would cluck her tongue at the choice: Wear pink, she used to screech at me when I appeared in something dark, wear pink!

Now the lizard was staring at me and I fought an impulse to shout for my grandmother. She needed her rest. Somehow I knew it was important not to be distracted, that I continue to paint steadily. I connected line to circles, connected my grandmother to Mrs. Narayan to the armless man to Nelson Mandela. I would even connect the nasty lizard as well, for it would make my grandmother well. It must make my grandmother well. For how would I live without the shade of my green hill? How would I travel, how would I transgress, how would I troubadour my life away if there was no hill upon which to rest my head?

My grandmother recovered that summer. Yama, the god of death, decided to stay away, and I stopped drawing mandalas.

Five

I loved wandering around in my grandmother's house. My great-uncle's room was always cool, with gauzy curtains over the open window. There were no windowpanes in Grandmother's house; insects flew in at will through the bars, and we all slept under mosquito netting. My grandmother had a room but I slept there, as did Jani, for Grandmother preferred the bench in the parlor for sleeping. We had a spare room for guests or to hang the washing in when it rained or on the days my grandmother went madhi—that is, super holy and untouchable until she had gone to temple and come back— her sari was hung by poles on lines high above the ground. The ceilings were twelve feet, and often I sat in this room, gazing at the madhi saris.

The parlor was airy, with plants and wooden

couches and cane chairs. There were carpets on the floor, old and thin with a few bare spots, but comfortable to the feet. There was a gods' room, filled with images and renderings of Krishna, Laxshmi, Pilayar, and other gods from the pantheon. Fresh flowers were collected daily for the shrine; every morning, my grandmother made fresh designs with rice flour for the prayers. I often sat with her during the prayers, my task being to ring the bell when the oil lamp was passed in front of the gods. My great-uncle practiced Yoga and performed his morning ablutions and rituals even earlier than Grandmother. He'd apply his caste markings with red paste and vee-buthi, a sacred powder made from elephant dung. He was a devotee of both Iyer and Iyengar customs, a follower of both Shiva and Vishnu, at least until noon each day.

There was a music room with a veena with a carved dragon's head in red and yellow at the end of its long neck, and a violin that Aunt Shalani could play on her visits. I don't know who played drums, but a mridangam stood in a corner. My grandmother said there used to be many musical evenings in the house when my mother was young. My mother's room and a small room with a writing desk and dusty trunks and wardrobes completed the house.

My grandmother told some stories about my mother to me. How when she was young, she could run like a pony, fast on her feet. How she liked to wear ribbons in her hair and wanted green ones for every birthday. My mother was born March 11, and the astrologists said hers was to be a special life.

Until I was fifteen, I had never thought of my family as sad. We were not wealthy, but my grandfather had been a structural engineer of some renown. My mother, of course, had stripped our family bare, and because of her ours was a family violated by scandal, indiscretion, and shame. It was like Phaedra wedded to the House of Athens; of course, even after her, the House endured. But while Phaedra had been cursed by the gods, my mother alone was responsible for her actions. So I thought. Our family shook like a tree after my mother's various transgressions. Once Jani and I attended a bharatnatyam recital in the city; as we were being seated, several acquaintances murmured a hello. It was then that someone whispered something about "those poor girls" and I realized our situation must look bad on the outside. I wanted to shoot the whisperer immediately.

My great-uncle, with his strange mannerisms and shaky past—a man whose nails were yellow with opium, whose head swam with drugs—did little to help us; he would get dreamy in the middle of the day. He liked to wear multicolored turbans. He thought Coleridge was the greatest poet ever and could recite "Kubla Khan" any time. My great-uncle was a thin, wraith-like man with a sweep of white hair that he sometimes pulled to a knot at his neck. I was twelve before I learned that he had been married, that his wife had been struck by a car and died. I couldn't imagine him married, any more than I could believe he had ever been a baby. I thought he had simply sprung from somewhere, fully grown and alone, born in a field of poppies with a pipe in his hand.

He was always lounging, a pillow behind his back, his legs completely relaxed. Even standing, he looked graceful, like a tall girl. His clothes all flowed. They rippled somehow, his shirttails long, his dhoti full of folds. Sometimes it seemed he didn't have any bones in his body. They said opium eaters imagine they can make their bodies so malleable that they can slip through the smallest spaces; my great-uncle seemed to be able to go anywhere, his body merely pretending to be flesh.

My great-uncle was a painter. He could paint miniatures of courtly scenes of times past very efficiently. He would bend over small squares of canvas and apply blue, green, and red paints with the tiniest brush. He was extremely disciplined in the morning. He got up at dawn, performed his ablutions, ate a spartan meal. Then for four hours, he would attend to his canvas, silently working. He sold about half through an arts association in town, his customers being largely both island-Asian and Chinese. He had a retrospective once in Taiwan. He attended the opening-day ceremony, but growing bored, he hurried home to Pi, to his paint and his opium.

"Careful," he'd say to me in Italian as I leafed through his works. "The gold will shake off the canvas if you are not careful." He painted dancing girls and musicians and once an unusual series of ordinary folk done in the courtly style, sweepers and villagers performing their daily tasks. He asked me to pose once, which caused a big ruckus with Grandmother.

I had one of his contemporary studies, as they were called, at home in Madras. It was of a schoolteacher with her pupils under a banyan tree. It gave me a sense of serenity. Through it, I saw his power, and I thought my family's strength was inextinguishable.

The gossips didn't think so. We were a family of women, without a strong man to give us buoyancy in the social waters of Madhupur. I didn't think we needed men. My aunts largely managed without them, and prospered. In fact, I think, without men we were stronger. No one to slap us into obeisance. Society required women to marry, and men were needed to father children. But once that occurred, wouldn't everyone be better if they vanished into their own worlds like my great-uncle, leaving women to conduct their lives? But my grandmother was worried about our reputations; she wanted to find a suitable boy for my cousin Jani to marry.

I looked forward to Jani's arrival. She would make me laugh and help me keep my anger toward my mother at bay. But Grandmother said Jani was reported to be forever frowning, clutching Christian books in her hands. Her eyes were listless and she would answer queries with monosyllables. "She's moody because she longs for a companion," my grandmother said, but I wasn't sure. What had happened to Jani?

I spent March at my grandmother's with a great deal of freedom. I'd rise late, read storybooks, eat lightly. I spied on my mother, as I've said, and made up stories to amuse myself. Often I took a chair to the field behind the house. I sat and watched the green grass, the dandelion fuzz at the edge of the field, the rough, high grass. Dragonflies speckled gold and green whizzed by, and fat bees sucked greedily from the nectar-laden flowers. Sometimes I could picture my entire life in the slow rise and fall of the field, the way it expanded so that I could see what was just in front of me really well but couldn't make out what was in the distance.

Mango trees and palms dipped with the wind, and sometimes you could hear the thud of fruit falling. The monkeys would claim it, take a bite, and throw it away. They were wealthy here and had more than enough to spare.

Jani arrived on a Saturday. At once I sensed something wrong. Usually she would fling her bags down and cover us with kisses. But this Jani was different, distant, her motions contained, her arms passive. She smiled and said everything was fine, only she was tired, could she go to bed? Grandmother and I were astonished.

Grandmother decided to go ahead and inquire for possible marriage partners for Jani. Through friends and relations, she located one, C.P. Iyengar. From his photograph, he seemed to be a likable young man, with a smooth face and smiling eyes. He played tennis, swam regularly, and had his degree in biotechnology. He also wrote poetry. I was impressed, and thought Grandmother might be right. He was visiting the island by chance (cosmic circumstance, my grandmother said), and I was eager to meet him, this tennis player from India.

Jani refused to talk about him, though. She simply shrugged her shoulders when I asked her how she felt about meeting him. I thought she was still tired.

Instead, I rattled off the many good things to look for in possible husbands, such as an interest in sports and dogs and tropical fish, a preference for Coca-Cola, and a good dress sense. I told her I would draw up a list she could use for reference, but she was uninterested.

With much reluctance, my cousin agreed to meet the family of the suitor Grandmother had selected. On the afternoon of the first visit, Jani dawdled in her room. She had put on her favorite blue sari, made of soft georgette with a simple dark blue border, but Grandmother thought it too plain. "You look like a schoolmistress," she said, advising a Benares silk. "But it is so hot," complained Jani, and the two of them argued for a long time. Finally a pink and white cotton was chosen, very fashionable but comfortable. My mother slipped out early.

If Jani had been going to a picture, she'd have outlined her eyes in dark pencil, piled silver bangles on her arms, and dabbled on perfume secreted from my mother's bureau. But for this afternoon, she just scrubbed her face and lingered in the room. When the visitors were announced, Vasanti merely crying loudly, "They've come!" my grandmother and I went to meet them. We ushered them in and settled ourselves in the drawing room. I sat on the sofa, opposite the sister-in-law. Only she and his brother came, preparing the way for a later visit from the parents and the boy himself. His brother looked a lot like him, and his wife had a big pink mouth and a blaring orange sari. She was from Bombay and spent a long time talking about her former home. They spoke almost in chorus, completing each other's sentences, and praised C.P. He was an engineer, very capable of securing a promotion and possibly would be offered a position in Canada. Grandmother frowned a bit over that, and sensing her hesitation over having Jani so far away, the wife assured us that it would be several years before that could come to pass. Vasanti brought us tea and cakes.

It was a pretty tray, with almond and silver frosted cakes, thick pieces of shortbread, Mysoor halvah, spicy nuts, murruku, and water biscuits. The tea was strong and hot, and Grandmother poured with grace. She gave me several pointed looks, for Jani still hadn't come down, but I ignored her. If my cousin needed extra time before meeting prospective in-laws, I was not going to hurry her. Instead, I reached for a second slice of cake and examined our guests. They were polite, spoke English with British accents, suggesting educations or vacations abroad, and were conversant on contemporary films and dance recitals. They questioned me on my studies, asked me what subjects I particularly liked, and were not surprised when I said science. We then spoke of favorite books, and I slouched a little, enjoying our talk. I liked these people, especially the wife, and thought that perhaps with a drink or two, the brother might not be so bad either. It was while I was thinking this that Jani finally came down. She was wearing the blue sari and her glasses, which she doesn't really need except for reading. She entered the room shyly, and at the last minute, tossed her head with indifference. Her face was settled into a mask, her eyes lowered, and her smile tight, as if acknowledging she was on display and that it wasn't going to affect her.

Conversation was awkward, with Jani answering their queries in monosyllables, and myself and Grandmother making up for the difference. When at last the sweets tray was taken away, and the silver dish of paan and slender cigarettes offered, the visitors seemed to suggest that they could not stay much longer. The wife invited Jani to tea at their house. "A simple affair, of course, but we might hear V. Lakshmi sing. Her singing is such a pleasure, don't you think?" I agreed heartily, although I hadn't any idea who V. Lakshmi was, and Grandmother glared at me while Jani for the first time seemed to smile. Grandmother accepted the invitation at once. I worried that their interest in Jani would fade if she didn't respond more enthusiastically to their queries. But even still and quiet, my cousin projected a powerful if somewhat guarded picture, and I think they were impressed. Stubbornness is a quality that runs deep in our family, the very quality that Grandmother warned us would leave us husbandless and sorry.

They finally left. We promised to come for their musical afternoon, and courtesies and compliments were paid. Grandmother was very excited.

"I think they like you very much, my dear," she said, giving Jani a little hug, "and you know, the blue is very becoming on you. Imagine them inviting us over so quickly; usually, they'd wait for a second interview. And the boy is very handsome, I hear, much better-looking in real life than in photographs. And did you hear her speaking so sweetly of her mother-in-law—yes, they are of very good family."

And Grandmother would have replayed the entire afternoon word for word, if Jani had not complained of a headache and gone to her room. So Grandmother talked to me as I retrieved the sweets tray and attacked the remaining cakes with relish.

"Not every family would be so open-minded about us. No male in the family, no parents. But our name is very good. Your grandfather was one of the most respected men in this town, renowned for his designs. They still speak of the Forest Building with respect."

My grandfather had designed the Forest Building for a Swiss corporation that was later taken over by Pepsi-Cola until it was banned from the island. It featured trees as pillars in the front and was now a government housing agency.

Grandfather had been an inventor as well, constantly busy with his hands. He developed a self-cleaning stove once but could find no backers. He said that women were destined to be chained to their housework if inventions were not created for them, but we all had servants to do the work and no one paid attention to him. Design those funny buildings, he was told, don't try to change the world.

On the day of the singing soiree, Grandmother made sure we dressed up and had fresh flowers for our hair. I adjusted Jani's jasmine and had her try on three saris until she chose the cream with flecks of gold and a border of large abstract mangoes and peacocks. It was an enchanting sari. Her bodice was long in the sleeve and cut attractively about the neck and back. She looked like a princess with her large bindhi—the mark on her forehead—and her regal stance. I was certain C.P. would flip over her. My mother, of course, wasn't coming. I don't think my grandmother even asked her.

We took an old rickety bicycle rickshaw because my grandmother didn't trust the motorized ones. Slowly, we pedaled our way to the other side of town, where the brother lived with his wife. C.P. was visiting them from Bangalore, where his parents had a large home. His father was in the timber business, managing ways for construction companies to locate and extract timber to house temporaries, people who visited the country on government business and departed quickly. He then went to do the same in other countries, and he made his way around Indonesia. The use of timber to build houses in India was very uncommon, since most architects preferred stone and concrete blocks. But timber was cheap, especially if it came from Thailand, and his was a thriving business.

The brother's house was built of concrete, a modern flat in a compound called Ashoka Gardens. It was painted pale pink, and the avenue it faced was lined with tall palms. We took our sandals off in the patio where we were greeted with a lush scent of incense that hinted of both tranquillity and money. About ten people had been invited, not counting us, and the parlor was filled with rustling silks. The flat was nicely decorated, in cool cream shades (thank goodness Jani's sari had a border or she would have melted into the background!) with large paper lamps and tasteful Mogul miniatures. A long

couch wound its way round in a vague semi-circular fashion, and the coffee table was teak, ornate, British Raj
influenced. The apartment had an aura of spaciousness
and quiet, typified by a large statue of Buddha in one
corner.

"Are they Buddhist?" I asked my grandmother who
merely frowned a negative. Hindus, then, like us, but the
family shrine was housed in the kitchen, off limits to the
guests.

C.P.'s parents came forward and cordially introduced
themselves and then introduced us to the boy himself.
He looked like his photograph and seemed vaguely embarrassed by the proceedings. The mother was warm and
effusive, the father jocular, and C.P. became unreadable.

We had some drinks (Grandmother again frowned
as I reached for a cupful of wine) and ate canapés made
of foreign ingredients—French cheese and apples. I
spilled some wine, Jani refused to eat, and Grandmother
all at once looked tired. Wiping up, settling down, we
watched as C.P.'s brother brandished a shining CD. He
popped it into a Bose stereo system, all sleek and silver,
and soon the melodies of classic Carnatic flute filled the
air. V. Lakshmi's voice was very high and lulling. It was
almost like being at a concert. I began to dream of Jani
and me running across a field, pursued by someone playing a flute. The field was endless, the sky a vibrant blue,
and our running effortless. The flute player fell away and
now we were running toward someone. Grandmother

nudged me awake. People were applauding, and for a moment I thought it was for me.

Yawning, I got up and selected a plate at a table brimming with desserts. I chose chum-chums and ba-dhushas, which were sweet and delicious, a perfect way to awaken. I met a young cousin of C.P.'s, about my age, who spoke of the test-match scores for the games be-tween India and the West Indies. I didn't follow cricket, but I liked talking to him, or rather, hearing him talk. He was cute, and I began to think this might be a very good family to marry into. I didn't have many friends who were boys, but I liked talking to them. I guess I was a bit of a tomboy, even though I read a lot. I liked playing at games but coughed a great deal if I overexerted myself. Anyway, this chap went on about cricket, and I listened, but my gaze wandered. Grandmother was talking to C.P.'s par-ents, possibly discussing jewelry, and C.P. was speaking to Jani. I couldn't tell if Jani was engaged in their con-versation; my cousin was inscrutable.

The boy was no longer talking of cricket, and I said something about the music.

"Boring, no?"

"No, I like it."

"You listen to pop?"

"I like some."

"I've got the Doors and Culture Club on CD. What about you?"

"I don't have any CDs, but I like the Beatles. And U-2."

"You like the B-52's?"

"Of course."

"Shall we put on some music?"

"They won't object?"

"Why should they?"

"Maybe they would."

"Do you think we shouldn't?"

"We should do it."

"Okay."

So we found a Beatles album and put it on, and no one minded, and this young boy and I sat down and listened to the music. I wanted to dance but thought Grandmother would have a fit if I did. Some of the guests did begin to dance, though, and since there was a crowd, the cousin, whose name was something I didn't catch, and I joined them. It was fun, the music was "Please Please Me," and I lost myself in its beat. C.P. asked Jani to dance. But stupidly, she wouldn't, and I wondered at this, thinking if Jani wouldn't dance with him, she wouldn't marry him either.

I remember thinking his family doted on him. They had served him food first and later listed his favorite foods to my grandmother. At one point, his father asked me what the young miss wanted to do when she grew up. I said I wanted to be a zoologist. He smiled indulgently.

"You like pop music too much to study seriously, perhaps? Would you not say that is the case?" he asked.

For some reason, I began to list colleges that Western pop musicians had gone to: Harvard, the London

School of Economics, Rhode Island School of Design. His son came over and said John Lennon had gone to art school. His father then pointed at a backgammon board that C.P. had made, handsomely marked with triangles in light and dark wood.

"Jani's a lovely girl," said the father. We looked at her talking to the sister-in-law.

"They're discussing sari shops. Think of it, two honor students talking of fashion," said the father. C.P. and I smiled. I told C.P. that I was reading Russian novels, and he told me to read *The Brothers Karamazov*. Guests began to disperse. Grandmother thanked our hosts, and we left for home.

Six

Jani refused to talk about the party. My mother read a book while I complimented C.P., hoping to get a reaction from both of them. I could tell that Jani and my mother did not get along. At least, if my mother had participated in a conversation like a normal human being, they wouldn't have gotten along. Jani dismissed my mother but never said anything to me directly, to save my feelings. But I could see it in the way Jani regarded my mother, the way her mouth would tighten, and her eyes, too, holding back, as if she were a snake, a hiss.

Animal behavior was a subject I liked. I remember reading about cats and birds. Cats don't like heights, things like that. Birds at a young age are inherently afraid of hawks and not afraid of geese. If a cardboard cutout of a goose is passed over their baby heads, they do not mind. But they are terrified by a fake hawk. Jani, I think, thought my mother was a hawk, and instinctively, her back went up, ready for a fight.

I think Jani saw my mother as selfish; at least she was alive and could talk to her daughter, that sort of thing. Jani missed her own mother terribly, I knew, for I had noticed how suddenly sometimes her eyes would become distant and full of sorrow. No one said that Jani was an orphan—in India, I don't think parenting is so exclusive that other relatives aren't involved in all aspects of raising a child, so the child is part of a community from the first—but she was sensitive, and felt the loss. When we'd see films about death and dying, her cheeks would wet with tears. Quickly, she'd try to dry her eyes in the cinema dark with the hem of her sari border but I noticed. In grieving for her mother, Jani also grieved for me.

My aunts did not do a bad job of raising me. There wasn't enough room, and we were in one another's way sometimes, the children and I. Usha practiced singing, which sometimes interfered with my homework assignments. I'd be trying to memorize species subgroupings, and there would be Usha trying to sing in Sanskrit. And Usha would want to turn the lights out to sleep before I did, because I wanted to read a novel in bed. So I used a flashlight, a tiny one no bigger than my elbows, and tried to read. But it was uncomfortable and threw the wrong shadows, and I wondered if it was worth the effort. But then I got used to reading in the semi-dark.

There were the occasions of illness. Bronchitis was the most common, followed by stomach flu, head colds, ringworm, hives, mononucleosis, and laryngitis. I got the measles, the mumps, and the chicken pox, despite the inoculations. They thought I was dying on at least two occasions. My aunt daily checked my temperature and always gave me an extra blanket; this made me sweat, and I think added to the odds of my getting sick the next day, due to the flux of sweat and chill in the air. I was always sleepy, or not at all sleepy, and my own body wearied me. But one of my doctors (I had three) told me early on not to succumb to depression and to keep myself engaged and alert, even when bedridden. That's why I read novels and studied a bit of zoology on the side (it wasn't offered at my school, but I picked up old textbooks from the book vendors).

We had one dog and two cats, but they were strays who had adopted us, and they slept outside. I liked them because if I missed school, they were my companions in a nearly empty house. I'd let the dog jump on my bed while I read and would try to fluff out the dog hairs from my bedding before my aunties realized the infraction of the no-dog-on-the-bed rule. The cats roamed at will. But all that was at my aunts' home in Madras.

Here on Pi, at my grandmother's house, I found myself rapidly becoming bored. Jani spent her time quietly reading. I had already gone through all the activities I had planned. Twice, I collected wildflowers and pressed them between the pages of the old *Pears Cyclopedia* in the hall. Twice, I sat with my watercolors, straining my eyes at the garden, trying to paint delicately and faithfully. I peered into the Italian grammar and studied for a full half hour. I read through all the "Humor in Uniform" and "Life in These United States" bits in the back copies of the *Reader's Digest* stored in the closet. I picked at a collection of abridged Dickens and longed for something to do. I took to wandering around the compound and making a nuisance of myself. Jani responded only in grunts to my whining. No one would play cards with me. My great-uncle was unavailable. I tagged behind my grandmother until she got tired and told me to make myself busy. Even my mother, usually good for an hour or so of spying upon, was boring; she was stretched out on a chaise longue, giving herself a clay mask treatment. The world was dull, dull, dull.

In exasperation, for I kept coming into the kitchen for something to eat, Vasanti sent me off to the market. I was given a string bag, rickshaw money, and a rapid goodbye. I decided to walk and save the fare for a flavored ice later on. The day was still cool. I passed a group of children playing hopscotch. I began to wish I had a special friend, a confidante. There were usually people like this in the books I read, girls who walked arm in arm, telling each other heart secrets. I didn't have any close friends at school, being absent a lot. The girls I admired ignored me, having their full share of friends. I must have appeared strange, half brown, half white, without actually having the cachet of having been to America. I always seemed the odd one out. Anyway, these girls liked silly music, teenage stuff, and had no interest in books, except romances. It was different when Jani shared her Mills and Boons romances, because we talked about other things. But the girls in my class seemed immature. I guess that's why I liked Jani so much—she never took me for granted.

One of the teachers befriended me, a pretty young English teacher named Miss Julie. She discovered my interest in reading and lent me many novels. She was careful not to show me special attention in class, and it never occurred to me to invite her to the house. When I told my aunts about her, they told me to ask her over for lunch, but I never did.

Once I met her on the street. I nearly didn't recognize her, so accustomed was I to seeing her in a classroom. But there she was with an armful of colorful bangles and sunglasses pushed to the top of her head. She was with a young bearded man whom she introduced as Mr. Vivek. She hesitated for a moment, but the man broke in and added that he was, in fact, Miss Julie's husband. My confusion must have broken out like a hidden sun on my face. "Yes," she said, "I've been married for a month or so. I thought I'd tell you next term, since we'll be finishing up so soon. You girls are so, so inquisitive."

I understood what she meant. The girls in our class, once they heard that Miss Julie was married, would crowd around her desk and tease her unmercifully. They would want to know all sorts of things, how handsome he was, how they had met, did she shave her legs before the wedding night and what else did she shave, things like that. I assured them that their secret was safe with me. Still, I thought she might have told us, so that we could have celebrated with her, brought her a gift, taken a half-holiday from classes.

Later, I wondered if Miss Julie had wanted to keep the marriage secret for another reason. Perhaps it wasn't approved of by her parents, or perhaps they were too poor to have a big wedding and were ashamed. It never occurred to me to doubt their word, for the idea of Miss Julie having a boyfriend seemed too ridiculous. Yet that was the very rumor that swept through the school the next term. She never mentioned her marriage to anyone.

But this was Pi, not Madras, where liberated Christian schoolteachers might have as many boyfriends as they desired. The island was off the coast of India, not connected to the mainland, an eye, a tiny eye, to the teardrop that was Sri Lanka. It had been invaded and colonized so many times that it nonchalantly absorbed the morals of every culture that came to it. Castes intermarried, racial lines were blurred, and nearly everyone was an eighth something else. I was certain my family had both African and Dutch blood in it somewhere, but that was of course hushed up. Anthropology would prove me right, but religion remained an obstacle. Our family descended from pure-blooded priests, said my grandmother firmly, refusing argument. As such, we had our own codes for conduct, and old traditions reigned. Thus, to our acquaintances with similar histories and beliefs, my mother was a tramp.

The marketplace was a mixing ground for rich and poor. There were big stores with shiny windows displaying the latest sari fashions and jeans and small shacks selling betel leaf. Women spread their wares on burlap smoothed over pavement; men set up wooden crates to sell imported watches and fancy scarves. Book vendors showed off their fare on rickety, movable stands, the spines facing out. I always took a long time choosing a title from my favorite book vendor. All the books were used, and many were in English. Some were from religious publishers, some were commercial, and some were from a local press that published poetry on handmade paper. There was always a supply of Penguin paperbacks, and I often walked away with a good Jane Austen or George Eliot.

I dearly loved this stall. The owner was a fat Turk

who wore an embroidered fez and a short crimson vest. He had a face that seemed to exist only for his smile, which left him a dimpled baby. He didn't mind how long I took with my selection, and sometimes let me sit on an old orange crate, reading a few pages to see if I liked the beginning.

But this day I didn't have money for a book, so I turned to the food stalls. I picked ripe tomatoes, plump lemons, and slender eggplant. I found fresh garlic and bunches of coriander. What else did my grandmother want? A packet of sugar and small white onions. Finally, I was done, and began to debate over a cold soda or slices of peppered mango. I opted for the latter and made my way to the stall that sold the sweet, juicy, yellow-orange fruit. There was a white man there already, ready to pay for his purchase.

"One rupee," said the owner.

"Not more than four anna," said the foreigner and I together. He and I began to laugh, and the owner shrugged.

"Let me buy you a slice for coming to my aid," said the man, sounding like an American.

I refused, saying it wasn't anything much. I noticed that he was older, about thirty, I thought, with short blond hair and green-grey eyes.

"I've been here so long, it's funny that someone would try to swindle me," he said so the vendor wouldn't hear.

I smiled and turned to buy my mango. When I turned back, he was gone. I was a little disappointed, for I would have liked to talk to him a bit. I didn't know any Americans, except for Mary Ann, a girl at school who said "okay" a lot. Wiping away the golden juice that dribbled over my chin, I made my way home. I passed a foreign couple, Japanese, in a cuddle. All around me, people were cuddling—Indians, islanders, Pakistanis, Singhalese. Was the world love-mad? Or had it always been this way, and I was just suddenly more acutely aware of it? March was warm, the tail end of spring. There were rains in the north, and we'd be getting our share of them in a few months. But the island seemed to be monsoon-crazy already, affecting couples with lovesickness early. "Cheap display," elder lookers-on would mutter, like in the song by Joni Mitchell. "Amour" would whisper others.

I had a book of Indian miniatures and was enthralled by the pictures of decorous courtly love, royal couples in royal pavilions, faithfully attended by respectful servants, always in a garden with a small deer or two in the background, trees dripping with leaves and fruit over the bower, a fountain in the foreground. I thought I would fall in love like everyone around me, respect my husband, and have many children. Someone I could look up to, someone tall, but not too tall. Someone I would cherish. Toting the groceries, I wandered home.

Seven

The next two days it rained. Everything was drenched.
There had been no news of Jani's suitor.

"Do you think you're in love with C.P.?" I asked, unable to stand Jani's silence any longer.

"Love? No, I don't think so," answered Jani.

"But could you grow to love him?"

"I don't know."

We were in our room, in bed, but not talking. Usually, Jani would tell me straightaway what was in her heart, but now she was on guard. She was afraid of something, and I dearly wished I could make it all right for her.

"Are you going to marry C.P.?"

"I suppose I have to—unless—"

"Unless what?" But she just laughed.

"Unless one of your heroes arrives and rescues me, I guess."

"Why can't C.P. rescue you?"

I wanted to rescue her. I was ready to be Jani's knight, to wear her favor upon my sleeve and fight for her.

"There's so much you don't know," she told me.

I guess it was true. One by one, Jani refused to meet any other suitors selected for her. At first she complained that she didn't like this one's nose, this one's hair, when she was presented with their photographs, but then she started to say nothing, becoming glum and silent. Grandmother became exasperated, sometimes trying to coax her nicely to give one a try—here, this one is a genius, and he is loved by his three sisters—but Jani would have none of it. Then Grandmother would lose her temper, stamp her foot, appeal to the gods. Jani would close her ears and retire with a devotional.

I became distracted by the rain. It pounded on the roof and gushed across the windows; the trees would sway back under its assault. I caught a little cold and had to stay in bed. Jani brought me trays of orange juice and toast. The entire household was a firm believer in bed rest and vitamin C. I was agonizingly bored.

"Come, now, it's not so bad," said Jani, but she didn't like to sit at the window while it poured and listen to the singing of the wind. She didn't like to lie under the awning of the balcony where the water dripped into saucepans and watch the villagers make their way through the puddles, protecting their heads with plantain leaves. Not for her the vibrant pounding that made you want to dance in imitation of the raindrops, plunk, plunk your feet up and down, and then thunk, thunk, thunk for thunder. Rain was something to avoid for Jani, something to come out from.

Surprisingly, my mother came once or twice to check up on me. She looked at me through the doorway, but if I attempted a smile, she didn't respond. Once she did smile at me, but it was my turn to pout and stew. All right for her to stand and smile, while I was bedridden. Where was she when I was well and able? I scowled quite fiercely.

When the days were bright again, I soon went back to the market. I brought along a book of zoology to a cafe I had lately discovered. It was a well-lit place full of scuffed tables and patrons who nursed their drinks for hours. I had a rose milk, which I took to a corner table by a window that poured in sunlight.

I liked what zoology offered me. In the study of animals, I saw how environment affects a certain species and what bearing it has on its life. I thought about Jani's upbringing, how she had no parents, how she seemed docile and able to adapt to any given environment. Her stubbornness in refusing even to be nice to C.P. must be the result of all that former adaptability. If Jani were an animal, her species would die out in her refusal to mate and create offspring. All Grandmother was trying to do was to continue the species.

I looked at my book of animal classifications. There

were nineteen categories of animal life before even getting to the class of mammal and man. If all the protozoa
and the mollusks and segmented worms reproduced regularly, why couldn't Jani? Even my mother followed the
biological urges that maintained mankind, although she
should certainly retire her wares by now. I expected to
marry and have children. Maybe I'd settle on Pi, in a nice
house with a garden, and work at the wildlife preserve in
Cootij. It was a place with lots of protected land and full
of options for a zoologist. I could come back from Radcliffe, get married, and go to work immediately. Idly, I
began to wonder who would be at my wedding. My sisters, of course, but what of my mother? I was interrupted in my musings by a tap on the shoulder.

"Hello, my friend," said an American voice. Turning
around, I looked up to see the American from the mango
stand. Wonderingly, my face grew warm.

"Hi," I said finally.

"I'm happy to say no one else has been trying to
swindle me," he said.

"That's good."

"Anyway, it's not like I'm wealthy or anything," he
said.

"But you're American—that's enough," I said. It was
true. America and money went hand in hand.

"What are you reading?"

I showed him my book, feeling a bit foolish. But together we looked at the insides of a great blue whale.

"I once went on a whale watch and saw a whale

breaching. It was magnificent; it leapt into the air, and it kept on emerging. It didn't look like anything I'd seen before," he said.

"Wow," I said.

It was the only response I could think of. I could say I'd seen a jellyfish, lots of seaweed, an eel or two, and once, a shark's carcass, but what were those next to whales?

"It was enormous. It's hard to imagine something so enormous," he said.

"Yes," I said.

"Are you studying for school?" he asked.

"No, I'm on holiday. I just like to read."

Seeing that my rose milk was almost empty, he asked if I wanted another one and soon joined me at the table.

"I was never any good in science. I liked music, though. I played violin for years. My mother wanted me to be the next great violinist; she was deaf to the sounds I produced. Treat it like an instrument, Richard, not like a device for torture, my teacher would say."

"My aunts used to make me take classical dance, until I finally convinced them it was a lost cause. I like music, too," I said. "I also like rose milk. Do you?"

"No. I like lassi, and buttermilk."

"I like curds and rice with cucumber and mustard."

"What I love are the bhajis, anything fried. It's not at all good for you, though."

"My grandmother is a stickler for healthy type foods. We never have bhajis."

"Well, maybe we should order some now."

I agreed, thinking it only a slight indiscretion.

Munching on the fried onions and potatoes, we talked some more. I liked the way he looked and the quiet shy smile. He didn't smile often, which made me smile all the more. He wasn't handsome in the way of a model or film star, but handsome in that his features were composed, his expression calm. I felt I could learn from him, although I didn't know what I wanted to learn. He was sexy, too. Sitting next to him, I found my attention wandering from what he was saying to the nice color of his shirt, his darkish whitish skin, the depth of his unfathomable eyes. Then I snapped myself out of this spell. He was just an American talking to a kid, me.

"What do you do, Richard?" I asked, testing out his name.

"I give English lessons to schoolboys. Not girls, of course, they're too shy. I came to India to study ayurvedic medicine, and I take classes here on the island."

"Do you have a lot of money?" I asked, not shy.

"No." He laughed. "The classes I take are free. Do you know Guru Gowmathi?"

I shook my head.

"He teaches all of us—there are six of us—for free, with the idea we will spread his knowledge."

I had heard of foreigners coming to study Indian arts but had never met one.

"Are you full Indian?" he asked me.

I told him my father had been white.

"Your features are just slightly different from most of the Indians and islanders."

I became self-conscious then and told him I had to go.

We parted when it began to grow dark. Thinking my grandmother would be annoyed that I'd stayed out so long, I hurried. As I walked along, I realized how starved I had been for a real conversation, that the person I knew most was myself. Talking with Richard made my heart light, and even the flowers around me seemed more potent. I was heady with excitement at the time I'd just had. He had seen a whale!

Fully expecting to be reprimanded at home, I was surprised at my grandmother's abstracted greeting. She yelled just a little, and then she urged me to see my cousin. I followed her to our room, where I discovered Jani weeping on the bed.

"She has been like this all afternoon," said my grandmother, wringing her hands.

She left me with Jani, and I approached the bed.

"What's wrong, Jani? Tell me what's the matter," I said softly, putting out my hand to stroke her back. But my words only made her weep harder, so I sat quietly.

"It's no use—I can't pretend," she finally said between sobs.

I stroked her long black hair, untangling the knots. She said I was too young to understand, that I couldn't comprehend. But I begged her to try, and slowly, she told me. She spoke of her friends, of Nalani and Rohini, both of them recently married, and how they told her that it hurt to give birth to a baby. How could they do this to her, Grandmother Kamala and our relatives, marry her off and subject her to such pain? I said, no, no, it's not like that, there doesn't have to be pain. I had read a lot more books than she, I told her, and I knew it didn't have to be so. I said, think of all the others, think of the drugs, think of most of the world, think of *The Good Earth* and how babies just dropped in the fields while the mothers worked. But Jani said that there were always some exceptions, that some girls never feel the monthly pain and some scream for hours, and what would I know anyway? I know, I know, I said, I know the thing between men and women, and how they fight for each other, how they brave fire and exile to sleep with one another, how they adore their babies. Jani, because she felt she had already told me so much and there was no reason to hold back, said she was really afraid of killing her baby. What can I do? she wailed. I won't be able to give birth! And if I do, the baby will die! You can't know that, I said, you can't possibly know. But Jani said there were some things you just knew about your body, and she was absolutely, positively sure.

I tried to calm her and soothe her, but she kept crying.

"I cannot marry C.P.," she said.

"You need to fall in love with someone," I offered.

"No one will ever love me, no one that gentle," she said.

"Maybe you don't have to sleep with your husband," I said, but even as I said that, I knew it was preposterous. Children were always the object of marriage; everyone knew that.

"There is only one thing I can do, and I need to do it soon," she said.

I became alarmed, and thought she meant to take her life, but she merely clasped a blue prayer book to her heart and closed her eyes.

"What will you do, Jani?" I asked finally, scared.

"I am going into the convent."

"Convent!"

"I'm devoting myself to God."

Eight

My grandmother took Jani's news badly.

"What do you mean?" she screamed.

"I'm better suited for a convent. I'm not made for this world," said Jani.

"Is it because you don't like C.P.? You don't have to marry him; we can look elsewhere."

"I don't want to look anywhere. I'm becoming a nun."

"And what about our gods? Are they not enough for you?"

"I've thought it over, and my mind and heart are clear," said Jani.

"Why do I have such strange girls around me?" moaned my grandmother, glaring at all of us, including my mother.

When Jani said she wasn't meant for this world, I was reminded of something else. A long time ago, something terrible had happened to Jani. A baby she was watching died. Little Jou-Jou was a cousin's baby, and Jani at ten was asked to keep an eye on her while the mother was gone. Jani sat in a chair and for five minutes watched the baby's face; Jou-Jou looked like an old woman with red eyes. Then Jani turned away and settled more comfortably in the chair, waiting for the mother's return. How unimaginable it was that when the mother did come back, her smile of thanks to Jani turned into a shriek; the baby's face was purple, its body still. It was one of those things that have no explanation. The mother, mad with grief and shock, grabbed Jani and shook her violently, screaming, "What have you done to my baby?"

Grandmother had first told me the story while combing my hair, shaking her head with the sadness of the world. Jani had never mentioned it, but I vaguely knew she was uneasy about babies.

Once, when an aunt unthinkingly offered Jani her baby to hold, Jani ran from the room. My grandmother had said that Jani was a delicate soul, a little different from the rest of us, having witnessed tragedy so young.

But to become a nun! I never imagined that Jani would leave us. Up to the very moment of her departure, I kept on thinking that something would prevent it. I watched, desolate, while she packed a suitcase. Her closet was full of brightly colored saris and blouses she no longer had any use for, gauzy scarves that she bequeathed to me.

"You're not taking your shawl?" I asked, fingering the violet and pink cashmere I loved.

"God will keep me warm," she said, surveying her sandals.

"But Grandmother gave it to you."

"I know."

"But she'll be offended. You can't leave it," I said, packing it into her bag.

She took it out, whereupon I fiercely put it back.

"You're being a pig," I said, ready to cry.

"No one asked you," she said, pleading.

We looked at each other.

"So you don't want to marry C.P. So what? You can be an unmarried teacher. You can take a job," I said.

"It wouldn't work. I want to get away from everyone."

"Grandmother's heart will give out—bang!"

"I'm trying to pack peacefully," Jani told me, exasperated.

"Sure. You think you're running away to sanctuary, but it's all a big lie. You'll be surrounded by a lot of fat old cows who'll make you scrub the steps and wash the pots and pans," I said.

"You're smarter than that."

"Well, C.P.'s going to get hurt. He'll probably shoot himself, like Heathcliff," I said, finally.

"Heathcliff never shot himself."

"Don't go, Jani," I whined.

"I have to."

"But I'll be so unhappy."

"You'll survive. It's not like in your books—life is not romantic. Grandmother will survive, C.P. will survive, and I will, too," she said.

That was the way Jani left us. That day the world looked bleak and awful, and I thought I would go mad. But she was right, of course. We would survive this crisis, only I didn't know it then. How hard it was for my young heart to hear it, I who believed that life was full of climaxes and conclusions, dramatic excess that could shatter or build like Shiva's terrible eye. According to Jani, few were burned by the eye; the world was made up of those who lived, those who picked themselves up after the crossfire, who got on with it.

Jani was declaring her lot with the common man, but I'd have none of it. I was fifteen and still wanted to believe that things were more exciting, that life was a brilliant and gorgeous jewel.

Grandmother and I consoled each other. We were both in tears.

"It's those nuns who put such foolish ideas in her

head," she said to me. "If only she would get married, see that there is more to life than sadness and sighs to waste and while away the hours with."

"But Jani explained once to me that religion is beautiful. That there is no difference between many gods and one god," I said.

"Of course there isn't. But to waste time with such philosophical notions instead of just tending to life itself. If you have a schedule, and my girl, you can learn from this too, if you have a schedule for your days to get up and receive the milk from the milkman, to make coffee for the household, to watch the servants who come to clean house . . ."

"What if you don't have servants?" I asked, remembering Jani had once told me that having servants was immoral.

"Okay, no servants, then you do the work yourself. You go to the market and buy vegetables and make a meal or two or three at once. You sweep the house, you cut some flowers to bring in, you wash the clothes."

"But all that is work," I said.

"Work is what will get you through the days."

"I'm going to college," I said. "I'm going to hire many servants or live in a fancy hotel when I'm grown."

"And what about me?"

"You can live with me."

"We were talking of Jani."

"What about her?"

"How it is necessary that she not throw her life away. Well, maybe this is a good thing. Maybe she will learn something from the convent."

"Maybe," I said, doubtful.

My mother's sari rustled ominously nearby. I wondered why *she* hadn't chosen a convent.

Nine

Jani's departure left me with almost no one to talk to, so I began to go to the market frequently. Often, I saw Richard there. We would talk lazily about our childhoods and mutual interests. He told me how he had once longed to be a space explorer, and I told him how I had wanted to scuba dive. One day, when I was especially feeling Jani's absence, he took me to visit his friend Maria. "She'll cheer you up," he promised.

We set off for the northern part of town, which was just encroaching on the suburbs. The lawns had a very manufactured look: short and clipped identically.

"Maria rents from an old dance instructor," Richard told me. We passed through the gates of a handsome house, and went down to a side path edged messily with rose bushes. We came to a small bungalow with green shutters and a door framed in jasmine. The plaster was peeling, making large splotches on the walls. A stone Buddha was placed near a potted banana plant near the door.

A woman with dark hair streaked with grey answered the door, her smile widening when she saw Richard and me. She greeted us warmly; evidently, Richard had spoken of me to her, a fact that gave me a curious thrill.

She led us to a room that was cluttered with things: little curios of dancing Shiva, images of Laxshmi, smiling Buddhas, plants that trailed, three or four fishbowls, shawls tossed over chairs, pillows studded with mirror work, everything speaking of a woman who had traveled quite a bit. There was too much furniture: armchairs and sofas crowding one another, coffee tables that were piled with large books and trinkets. There was a clash of color permeating her home, chintz fighting with plaid, stripes overlapping flowered fabric. I was used to a more streamlined look from my family's houses, but I supposed Maria's place was very cozy to her, warm, with red and orange colors. One table held a typewriter and paper, an oasis amid the mess.

She fetched us a tray loaded with sweets and savories and a tall pot of tea. She urged us to eat and helped herself as well. I couldn't stop staring at her. She had an air about her that seemed to encompass freedom, and this wasn't just because she didn't wear a bra. She seemed more comfortable with herself than the women I knew.

Only my mother had her air of carelessness, but while in my mother there was an undertone of defiance, in Maria there was only generosity. She had lived on Pi for four years and had known Richard for three. She and her daughter had traveled all over the map before setting off for Asia. Now her daughter was in London with her father, while she continued to write "silly romances" on the island.

I felt privileged to meet her. I liked her because to me she seemed at once like someone you could trust. She told stories of meeting Richard when he looked bedraggled and carried a backpack.

"And look at you now, terribly respectable."

Richard blushed, and I felt happy.

Richard told Maria that I wanted to go to Radcliffe.

"You want to leave the island? And India itself! How can you?"

"I want to try someplace new," I said, realizing after the words were out that I sounded like Jani.

Maria seemed to think it was like running away. She told me that America might not hold such a sweet life.

"Do not put your life on hold, or wait until you escape to another world to start living your life as you want. While it is true you might start another stage, another phase, you cannot ignore the life you are in. I say this because I used to put my life on hold constantly. I used to say, when I get a car, I can enjoy the museum in the next town. This instead of merely taking a bus to the museum. After I lose weight, I'll buy the red dress. It's a Western notion, this idea of punishment and reward. Guru-ji tells us what the hippies used to say: Be here now. But enough lecture," she said, sitting back.

"No, go on," I urged, wanting to hear more.

"People always think they can start anew in some new town. But every time you move, you are either running toward something or running away from something."

Then she stopped and began to laugh.

"I should talk, look at me here."

"Were you running from something?"

"My husband, yes, my old life, my old friends. I thought Pi could answer my need to launch a new life."

"Has it done so, do you think?"

"It is different, yes, and I don't tire of it. At least, not yet."

"Maria is the most contented woman I know," said Richard.

We ate more snacks and drank more tea. Maria described her books, fairy tales retold as romances set all over the world. Essentially girl meets boy, girl loses boy, girl and boy find each other in the end. The same theme as found in the Tamil and Hindi popular films. She showed us the galleys for her latest, called *Last Hope, Last Time*. It was scribbled over in blue pencil, accompanying her editor's notations.

"I'm wildly successful. It's so odd because I came to

Pi to simplify my life, and yet I've had fortune beyond my expectations."

She told me that she had begun writing in the eighth grade, that she had tried her hand at protest plays in Oklahoma and then New York, but the audiences were small and there were always squabbles among the actors. She taught drama for a while in a community college but gave that up when her daughter was born. She was writing romances when her husband asked for a divorce, and two years later, she moved to Pi. Friends of hers had recommended it to her as a restful tropical island and had told her also about Guru-ji, a meditation leader and a follower of Maharishi Mahesh Yogi. At first I thought it was the same guru that Richard had spoken of, but I soon realized my mistake. This guru just led Yoga and classes on breathing and also performed some religious functions.

It occurred to me that foreigners latched onto gurus when they came to the island because it gave them a sense of community and some direction to their lives in a foreign place. Maria told me she was a Buddhist, a practitioner even in the United States, when the conversation veered toward religion. Foreigners liked to speak of religion more than islanders did, I thought, but maybe that wasn't the case.

My own beliefs were varied. Raised a Hindu, I took part in the daily prayer and ritual in my aunts' household and in my grandmother's home. I grew up with the images of the idols, and loved to hear the stories about them over and over. I didn't dwell on ideas of God and religion, though; it was just a part of ordinary existence.

I thought of Jani, and all of that Christianity, that Catholicism contained in her. Where did it spring from? My schools in Madras and hers in Delhi were either Catholic, nondenominational, or Muslim. In our books in English, the writers often wrote of Christians and heathens, and in my thirteenth year, I realized that I must be a heathen in their eyes. It was a shocking discovery and made me leery of Christianity. But Jani was be-friended by one of the nuns at her college, Sister Ava, who gave her a Bible.

The Bible was illustrated, and Jani showed me the pastel renderings of the Holy Family. I thought Mary looked a little like Jackie Kennedy, dark haired, elegant, noble. There was a story about a good Samaritan who helped a fallen man, and Jani told me about his piety in helping strangers. She made Catholicism sound attrac-tive, but still I wanted her to believe in Hinduism, in our gods. Gently, Jani admonished me, asking, "Aren't all gods equal?" Modern Hinduism, after all, absorbed Jesus into its fold, Buddha too, and Muhammad.

When I had earlier spoken to Richard about it, he talked of Existentialism, of the nonbelief in God. Athe-ism and Agnosticism. He believed in a higher power, but not in organized religion as manifested in the twentieth century, or even in the Middle Ages. I had read of the Middle Ages in the West, and told him that I admired King Arthur and Galahad and the quest for the Holy Grail, but I still liked Hinduism best.

"That's equally offensive as not liking Catholicism."

"But I do like Catholicism."

"But you like Hinduism best."

"Yes, but—"

"But what?"

"I don't know, Richard. I think it's dangerous to step away from the religion in which you were raised and embrace something new."

"Maybe it's the danger that attracts Jani."

"But she's scared of marriage!"

"She wouldn't be the first. Maybe she chose the Catholic God and the convent to safely unleash all the terror inside her. Maybe she could only express her courage by running away."

And then I thought of my mother and the possibility of her courage in running away from me. Maybe I represented domesticity to her, responsibility, yet how was this courageous? Running away seemed cowardly.

"The *I Ching* speaks of retreat, the courage to know when to step back from battle and gather strength before reentering the fray later," said Richard.

Richard spoke a great deal about the *I Ching*, a yellow-bound book about great knowledge achieved through change. It was printed in the Bollingen series by

Princeton University Press. One of my aunts had a copy; sometimes we kids used it as a fortune-telling game, opening the book randomly after posing a question. I knew that "Pi" for instance in the *I Ching* meant "grace."

"A period of grace in one's life," explained Richard. "That's why this island is special."

I agreed, although my mind was still on Hinduism and Catholicism. We approached Maria with the argument; being Buddhist, perhaps she could be detached and neutral.

"Religion takes different forms, and all gods are the same God," she said, bringing us more to eat.

"What about your daughter, what religion is she?" I asked.

"She is not Buddhist. I don't think she subscribes to any particular religion. She's dating a Jewish boy, and I think they attend services together."

"Where would she stand on this issue?" I asked, not wanting to let it go.

"Well, the Western notion is to choose your own religion, make up your own mind. So perhaps she would say Jani has the right to choose Catholicism. Whether she's right or wrong to step away from Hinduism, it is her own choice," said Maria.

"Hinduism accepts all religions," I repeated, wanting very much to defend my religion.

"But it refuses to accept converts," said Richard. "You have to be born a Hindu."

"At least it doesn't have rice missionaries, bribing the poor with food for conversion."

"And what about the corrupt priests?"

I don't think we came to any big conclusion, just that we spoke of it, something that perhaps my aunts would frown on. Religion and politics are best kept to one's own self, they felt, even though our family had taken part in the Freedom Movement in India and was vocal about its choices then. But that was a special occasion, they'd say; the matter is closed. Yet another door shut.

I thought about fate, how it cast us into different religions, mostly inherited.

"Of course, if one didn't believe in fate, one could say we choose our own boxes of religion," said Richard.

"As a people, we stand in our boxes and shout at one another. Until one box breaks, one rule gets broken, one religion pursues another," said Maria.

My mother broke the rules twice at least, once to couple with a North Indian to produce Savitri, and once to couple with an American—an American *something*—to produce me. Such transgressions lead to bad consequences, my neighbors would say, if not in this life, then the next. I wondered if I would be held accountable for her actions. Where had I heard that daughters were born to punish mothers for past sins? Already, I was a bit of a pariah at school for being illegitimate, and I knew that when the time came for me to marry, my mother's reputation would be an obstacle for the boy's family. Hinduism had strict codes of conduct. Yet my mother didn't seem to feel guilt. She just didn't care.

"Sonil."

With a start I realized I had drifted away from the conversation, and smiling, ate a sweet.

Ten

Thoughts of Richard often occupied me the entire day if I did not see him. I didn't understand this at first, and wondered why it was so. I tried to think about other things, but my mind was disobedient. I had grown used to his slow smile, his slouch as he sat, his American jeans. I felt embarrassed, as if everyone around me could guess at my thoughts. My grandmother didn't notice my distracted air, so distressed was she at Jani's departure. She began to devote herself to the garden and mutter under her breath. My mother of course ignored me, and in any case, she was not often at home, having found someplace else to fritter away her afternoons.

When Richard first invited me over to his flat, I didn't want to go. I was comfortable with the cafes, the visits to

Maria. To see him at home would seem strange. I reluctantly agreed.

He rented rooms above a restaurant that specialized in North African food. It was in a part of town which was half American and half French, most of the people belonging to a local ashram. There were some islanders, too, mostly college students who preferred cheap rents and the Western atmosphere. He took me to see the ashram.

It was a quiet place with one courtyard, a walled-in garden, a tiny fountain. The bowl of the fountain, its pond, was completely covered in rose petals that rested on the surface of the water. Richard and I sat at the edge. He dipped his hand in the water and drew out a petal. He tucked it behind my ear as I became perfectly still, holding my breath, alert.

We returned to his flat. It was clean, spacious, with only a few pieces of furniture, and crates of books everywhere. His bed was a mattress on a webbed frame, covered with a rough Indian-print cloth.

I can still remember that afternoon as clearly as if it happened yesterday. I remember pausing at his doorstep and slowly undoing the straps of my sandals. I remember lingering over this task, lining up my sandals just so. Barefoot, I stepped inside onto the tiled floor. I stood in front of a bookshelf, reading the titles on the spines. Turning, I found Richard right behind me, reaching to take my hand, and my reaching, too. I can remember the scent of the English-milled soap he used, the dampness of his just washed hair. "Let's eat," he said, and I blushed.

He made me pancakes in his kitchen. His father had taught him when he was eight, before I was even born. He mixed eggs and flour, honey and milk, added vanilla and sour cream, and poured circles into a hot skillet. He flipped them with ease and served them to me with real maple syrup. "It's from Vermont," he said, a place that to me sounded as exotic as Paris. Syrup burst around my fork as I pushed it through the spongy surface. It tasted wonderful, foreign, rich.

Then we had grapefruit. I was horrified to discover that he ate the inner membrane, the thick white threads and tough skin. I taught him to peel away the skin so only the soft, juicy, jewel-like pieces of fruit were revealed, to suck them away from their frame. My fingers wet, I fed him the choicest bits.

He kissed my mouth full of grapefruit tenderly. Swallowing, I kissed him back. I pressed my mouth all over his skin, sipping at his neck, his throat, his eyelids. I felt dizzy, transported, in another world. I didn't have time to think about what was happening, I just knew that my body was responding to his urgently. "We need some music," he said, smiling.

We sat cross-legged listening to a famous veena player on the radio. When the music started I forgot myself. I knew

I was in a room, that it was late afternoon, but here was this exquisite sound that seemed to carve steps in the air, on which I was ready to place my heel and toe and climb, climb for as long as it was required of me. Richard seemed as if in a trance; so inward was his gaze that I just closed my eyes and leaned back. I must have been lying there for a long time, my shoulders, my legs all soft, and I must have been dreaming, for the music had stopped, and here was Richard kissing me awake. I began to kiss him back, and he drew me to him, and I curved to him until it was like music, no end or beginning, just this feeling of body to body, his mouth, my mouth, his shoulder, my throat, my breast, my little baby breast, his smooth stomach, his tummy, his thighs, my tummy, my thighs, until he put his mouth on me, and it was the most lovely sensation, as if a thousand eyes inside me were slowly being opened.

Eleven

Now began a period of my life when the days were long and thick with desire. I lied to my grandmother that I had made new friends. Every afternoon, I met Richard in town, and we made our lust-soaked way to his apartment. But there was a world outside his four walls, full of gossipy mouths and lingering glances. I think because we made such an unlikely couple, however, and because of the distance between our ages, we did not attract too much attention.

The cost of seeing Richard was not something that I took for granted. It meant that I had to lie to everyone and sneak away to meet my lover. I had to plan and carry out the logistics of our trysts. It was thrilling. Not all of our meetings were full of unbridled passion; sometimes we just talked or listened to music. Sometimes we went for walks, but always I was afraid someone I knew might see us. Yet I loved to have my hand held suddenly, just as I was thinking that it was Mrs. Narayan I spied in the distance.

Once we did meet C.P.'s sister-in-law. We had not heard from her family since Grandmother had the unpleasant task of informing them that Jani had gone to a convent. The sister-in-law was surprised to see me in the company of a white man, or maybe just in the company of a man at all, or maybe she was just surprised to see me.

"The zoologist," she said. I had forgotten her name, so merely presented Richard. And I had forgotten zoology during these past days of my involvement with Richard. I did not pay much attention to the conversation. At some point, we said goodbye and continued with our walk.

Over and over, I saw him, I felt him. I remembered everything. If he rose to fetch us mineral water, or sometimes wine, I'd lie in his bed, in the warmth, and find myself blushing. It was like in the books, and sometimes I'd tiptoe over to the mirror and see if I could see any change; I'd run my hands over my breasts, feel the groan down there, but I still looked like myself. And when he finally climbed the stairs with the slender green bottle of divine liquid, I'd wrap myself immediately around him, in the open doorway, no shame. You are a beauty, you are bella, bellissima, beauté, my world, my love . . . he'd whisper, words I completely believed, words I wanted to hear again and again. I grew dizzy, I gulped for air, I could not separate my dreams from my waking life. I wanted to remain in bed forever, I wanted to do it, it, infinitely.

There's a Bob Dylan song, "I Want You." You feel he's singing with his heart, but also with his member. You know it is a song of ultimate longing. We made love to everything, the complete Dylan, old-fashioned punk, Talking Heads, and once, without paying attention, to the entire *Bangladesh* album.

Of course, it had to end. He said, I'm pretty old for you. He didn't say, you're too young. He said, you weren't even born when my parents would take me Queens to eat cheese blintzes with my grandparents. You weren't born when I hit a grand slam and broke Mrs. Moskowitz's window. You were a baby when I first read Vonnegut and Hesse and went to my first rock concert. You were a kid when I took Carolyn Maisel to the eighth-grade prom, and my brother told me his class never had dances because they were all hippies then. And on and on he went, hypnotized by the fact that he had been alive, and I had not.

I went to live with my aunts in Madras while he was a junior counselor at sleepaway camp in the Poconos. I was playing hopscotch when he decided to come to India and discovered Eastern religion. When he came to the island I was in grade school, having my hair braided in two parts.

I was already smarter. He was still reading Hesse, I was reading Tolstoy. He was a B+ student; I was straight A's. I knew I would do better than he had on the College

Board exams. But he was an adventurer, more experienced in life, while I was merely school taught.

I told him about my father. I imagined him a cowboy, and Richard laughed. "There are no more cowboys, Sonil," he said. But I believed my father had been a cowboy, someone who wore checkered shirts and pointy boots, who someday would rescue me from my mother. I worried I would take after her. Everyone said I resembled my father, having his hair and mouth. I was too anemic-looking to resemble my mother, who always seemed years younger than she was, with glossy thick hair and pearly teeth. My hair had been cut so many times for sickness that I wore it short. My grandmother told me that I looked like Louise Brooks, a favorite actress of hers, but I thought I resembled Alfalfa, one of the Little Rascals. "I love Alfalfa," said Richard, kissing my hair, but I wasn't sure. "Tell me more about your father," he asked.

"Okay, my father. I think he lives in Montana." I thought of Montana, what it represented. I had looked at a photograph once in a library and saw a sepia-colored sky and sepia-colored grass. I saw farm buildings set in a great expanse of grassland. Prairies. I liked the sound of that word. In America, I thought, I would learn. I would see what Willa Cather had seen. I had read *Death Comes for the Archbishop,* and I liked that story, all about a priest and his guide making their way through vast areas of land, helping the poor.

My English teacher, Miss Julie, had told me about the importance of the word, of language, of music, of invention, of giving yourself over to love. She asked me to read Cather and the Romantic poets, to read books about freedom—*Bury My Heart at Wounded Knee*, Sarojini Naidu.

"I once wanted to be a cowgirl," I said.

"A cowgirl?"

"A girl who wears a cowboy hat and a kerchief around her neck, who rides a horse and lets fly a lasso, who can ride with a herd of cattle."

"The wild cattle of Boston?"

"In Oregon or someplace. I wanted to be a trailblazer."

"You are a trailblazer," he said, kissing me. "So why not just go to the Wild West?" he asked.

"Radcliffe first, then the Western states."

"How do you know so much?"

"I study," I said quite seriously.

"And you read newspapers?"

"And I listen to music."

Richard told me about a music teacher he'd had early on who'd shown him the light.

"She was black. She taught us spirituals. One day she asked each of us in the class how many black friends we had. When it was my turn, I said, 'None.' I felt bad about that for a long time. My world was so white.

"Later, I began to question Judaism, and I started

to read about India, about China, about Japan. I even turned to Christianity and Islam, wanting to tie all the religions together with music. Every church, every temple, celebrates with some kind of song.

"I came to India because I wanted to learn to meditate, and I wanted to meet a holy man. I wanted purpose in my life. When I did meet a holy man, I had been on the island for sixteen months. He told me to teach English to young students and maybe contribute a tape machine to the temple."

"Did you?"

"Did I what?"

"Buy them a tape player?"

"A Sony with auto reverse."

We spoke about color. Richard disliked his white skin, which seemed even whiter when we held hands. He thought I wanted to be white.

"But I'm half white already," I said.

"I think you'd like to be all white."

Maybe he was right. I read white books, tried to dress more white than brown. And in being with Richard, I felt I was choosing white over brown. Yet I liked his whiteness, the sense of other in him, the foreign, the mysterious. I liked to place my hand next to his and compare the difference. But I didn't quite forget my darkness, my color, my *me*.

Sometimes, I told Richard, I got very anxious. I feared I would be left out of whatever was exciting in the world. There was a line in *Mrs. Dalloway* that always made me breathless. I had copied it out in one of my notebooks. She had gone up in the tower and left them "blackberrying in the sun." It made me ache, some solitary soul climbing dark, dank steps to a narrow room with a narrow bed while her companions have sun at their backs, purple juice staining their chins and hands. It was too awful. I resolved never to enter that tower, but to spend my days blackberrying. There were so many months of the year I stayed in bed, shut up like a Victorian invalid, having food brought up to me on trays, reading, reading until my eyes swam with tears. I was sick of it, sick of my room, sick of my sickness, sick of the pitter-patter of my aunts' steps as they stole in for just one more glance, one more peep, as if I were dying, a delicate china doll whose bloom had gone. No! I wanted to be in the fields, never mind my desire for whiteness, my hands scratched and bleeding from the brambles yielding the divine berries, the sun at my ankles, my hands purple. I wanted to defy them with the darkness of my skin, my aunts whose idea of beauty was a pale complexion bought in jars of "Miracle Turmeric" vanishing cream. I wanted to do a blackberry dance, color my face violet and stamp my feet in wine-making rhythm, exalt in the sun and spin naked.

"Spin naked to me, my blackberry beauty," whispered Richard. So I did.

Twelve

Jani wrote from the convent on thin foolscap with a smooth ball-point pen. I guess I must have expected her to scribble with a piece of charcoal or burnt wood, but then, I reminded myself, she was not in a prison, merely a nunnery.

Dear Sonil,

I am sorry I left so suddenly, but there was no other course of action I could take. It is nice here. I have met the novices, and other girls like me who just need a place to be. Some are expectant mothers thrown out of their families, and it is shocking to see how young they are. You and I have been very protected. Everyone is nice. Our days are full, from sunrise to sunset, with chores like cooking, gardening, repairs, and washing. The nights are hard, for I find it dif-
ficult to sleep. I lie awake and look at the curtains. A power-

ful nightlight makes shadows of pouncing tigers on the fabric, and the trees shake hard in the breeze. It is an eerie noise, like crying.

Here I feel very alone, not sure of anything, and see my own mortality every night. I have spoken to Sister Bernard about this (she is in charge of us new girls), and she says I must trust in Our Lord and has given me some prayers.

I say them, but my mind is still tormented. It will pass, though, as I gain more faith in Our Lord, and soon I will be able to sleep at night.

I like the quietness of my life here in the daytime. I tend to the vegetable garden where we grow the foods we eat. I cannot tell you the joy of watching the green leaves grow, the busy indication that the fruit is ripening. You and I like the market in town, but Sonil, there is nothing like pulling a tomato off the vine, the fuzzy prickliness of the stem, the way it drops—plop—so neatly off into your hand.

We have silent time like you thought we might. It is very pleasant to close one's mouth and not worry about words, especially in the presence of someone else. We're so compelled to speak all the time, to constantly shout at one another, we utter such senseless things. The joy of being around two, three, even five people at one time and not saying anything is so sustaining I look forward to it.

I hope you are not too lonely and are finding something to occupy your time.

Your loving cousin,
Jani

Jani's letter worried me. That she couldn't sleep seemed troublesome, indicating a unquiet mind. What was tormenting her? Was it merely what she should do with her life, or was she haunted by the specter of the past, like the baby that died? In turn, I wanted to tell Jani about Richard, but when I wrote back, I just spoke of the daily goings on in the house, about Grandmother's health, and so on. I told her about our great-uncle, who had not been home for several days. No one is worried, I wrote, for he is probably curled up asleep on a tattered couch in a hazy den in town. I didn't mention my mother.

Richard, Maria, and I went on a picnic. Richard drove a borrowed car, and I sat beside him, Maria in the back. We drove with the top down, the breeze in our hair, speeding past all the other cars through town. We passed a red Fiat full of college boys who honked and hooted, and it felt good to be going that fast. Soon, the town was behind us, and the open fields, wet with rice, were at our sides, and groves of trees full of monkeys with captive fruit in their mouths. We stopped at a grassy bank and ate chapatis filled with onion and potatoes and ripe tomatoes. We drank chilled bottles of ginger beer and passed around a joint. We napped in the sun. When I woke up, Maria was packing up the picnic.

"How are you getting on with Richard, Sonil?" she asked.

"Fine," I said. "Why?"

"I just wondered. I've known Richard a long time and have seen him with a few girls. He's like a little brother to me, and I want good things for him."

"You don't think I'm a good thing?"

She laughed, "You're young; your life is just beginning. Richard, well, he's young, too, and he doesn't yet know where he's going in this world. I don't know, I probably sound like a mother hen. I just worry about the two of you."

"Did you have many boyfriends after you left your husband?"

"No. At first, I kept to myself. Then I began to date younger men." She hesitated, then went on. "Richard and I dated for a few months. No, don't look like that— it was not serious. We were both lonely and scared of being alone. We're just good friends now. I got busy with my books. I think my big love is still out there, waiting for me."

"My mother is alone, too. Sometimes I think she'll marry again."

"How would you feel about that?"

"I don't know. She never speaks to me. Maybe she'll go away. She's already so distant. It's like I don't exist for her."

"Maybe you remind her of her past."

I said nothing. I was still thinking of her and Richard.

"Maybe she's just waiting for the right moment to speak."

We took turns trying to tickle Richard awake with a leaf. I remember that day clearly. Maria wore a turban, which she said was French. It was a hat that shaped up and sat square on her head, while her dark curls dangled beneath the rim. Her skin was tawny, her eyes brown, Semitic and large. Melting, I thought. She looked like a painting by Matisse. It was one of the happiest days of my life.

"I dream of you," said Richard. "I dream of you when I have coffee at the cafe. I dream of you when I buy a paper downtown. I dream of you at night when you are not beside me. I dream of you when I go marketing and pick up fresh, plump tomatoes. I dream of you whenever I eat mangoes. I dream of you when my mouth is full of your hair. I dream of you——" But here he stopped and broke off, thinking I was only a kid, a child, that he could not overwhelm me with the weight of his love and desire. He thought that if he told me things it would affect and change me. I didn't know how to tell him that my feelings were already too big.

Juliet. Lolita. Beatrice. I said their names like charms to make myself believe there was nothing wrong with being in love at fifteen. To love someone as old as Richard was not at all correct, I knew, but I did not know why. My grandmother was married at thirteen. At thirteen, they dressed her in bridal red, hennaed her feet and hands, and placed her in a flower bower with my grandfather. I don't know when they actually set up house together, at what point he walked up to her and untied the knot in her sari, but surely she wasn't older than fifteen. In two years, she would give birth to my eldest uncle. Kirti, the servant girl, was very young, and I knew she had a lover. So why was I so tormented? Because my desire was so big.

I think Richard made me feel powerful in some way. I liked the fact that he could reduce—or elevate—me to a being whose actions were dictated by passion. And that I could do the same to him. It was as if we both had a private world, with the larger world shut out. Our passion defined us, made us whole and real to each other. I was fifteen, and he was thirty, but he looked younger. Twenty-six. Twenty-six would make him eleven years older than I, but thirty made me half his age. Half his experience, half awake.

I think I thought sex meant love. I had become naked with him, to him. He had seen what no one else had seen. That made him powerful and made me his love slave. I could see the color-comic headlines: "Seduced by a Stranger," "Undone by a Hippie."

I had Richard, my cupcake of happiness, my deep-sea fantasy, my afternoon-love-affair man. And in my depth of feeling for him, in the enchantment of first love, first lust, I forgot my mother. Her evasions, her indifference, ebbed away. Here was a man who charmed me with attention, who marked me with significance. Here was someone I could love, someone who loved me.

Thirteen

This was how things were for a few weeks. But then the mad preacher came to town. I saw him on the streets. He wore a leopard pelt over his dhoti and had long, matted hair that reached past his shoulder blades. He was very, very dark, his skin nearly matching the color of his hair, and he was the most beautiful man I had ever seen.

For a few days he just stood in the street, silent and only partly in the way of the cars, the motor bikes, the bullock carts that were always about. The rumors declared he was from Delhi, that he was from Sri Lanka, that he had traveled to Pi from the heart of the Himalayas. From our favorite cafe, Richard and I watched him. We were both fascinated.

He stood in the street with his arms hanging straight down his sides, like some giant Egyptian statue. He had a multicolored bag across his shoulder, a glittering thing stitched with jewelstones and mirrors, embroidered with beasts and birds. A peeling harmonica peeked from the inside. He wore no shirt; he wore no shoes.

Drawn by Richard and the preacher, I returned to the cafe day after day. On the third day, he began to speak. He said that something grand had happened. He said the world was ripe for a miracle. He said he had another baby Jesus growing inside his chest. He removed his bag and thrust out his chest so that we could all have a look. A crowd of passersby peered at him, and we were among them.

His name was Be've'nu, and he did not believe in bathing, I thought, for a strong smell came from him. It wasn't unpleasant, but sweet, kind of smoky. Black hair curled sparingly on his chest, and on the left side was the outline of a tiny hand, almost a sketch.

"I was once a man like you," said Be've'nu, letting everyone get up close. Strangely, his accent was French.

"I slept at night, worked in the day, until one morning I felt a great pressure in my body. It was as if I had swallowed something and could not get it down. I tried to cough, spit it up, but the feeling persisted. Finally, I put my hands to my neck, sick of the pain that was so agonizing I wanted to choke myself. But I heard a voice that stopped me."

His voice was soft and full of wonder, his eyes round as he described the miracle that had befallen him. He spoke of touching the tiny hand that was on his chest, of his astonishment as he realized that a baby was inside him. The voice told him that it was another avatar of God, and that Be've'nu's life would change.

The baby spoke to him at night, telling him to gather up his life in a bag made by his own sister and to walk barefoot until sunset. Then he was to immerse himself in the first body of water he saw, whether at a tap or in an ocean. He was to abstain from food for three days and to chant the name of God. He was to stalk a leopard and kill it with his own bare hands, a knife in his teeth, and to sacrifice the meat, keeping the skin as a trophy. He was to walk from village to village and relay the miracle that was the life inside his chest.

Hardly anyone in the crowd believed in another Jesus, but his voice, the sweetest I'd ever heard, was captivating. Soon he closed his mouth and offered nothing more. The crowd, disappointed—the crazy who had appeared two weeks before had let a basketful of snakes travel up and down his arms—dispersed. Luck brought this preacher who was thirsty for water near our table.

"Where are you from?"

It was Richard who asked this question, startling me with its directness.

"From a road that's rapidly aging," replied Be've'nu.

"How did you get here?"

"I walk out on my own, a thousand miles from home, but I do not feel alone."

"How do you live?"

"You don't need a weatherman to see which way the wind blows."

He spoke only in Dylan. He did not use any other words except to tell his miracle. If I supplied mental guitar and harmony, it was like being at a rock and roll concert.

I went to lie in Richard's arms that afternoon. The heat of the day made us drowsy, and as I drifted off to sleep, I imagined it was the dark one's arms that held me, that the preacher's wild hair lay about me, that it was his face I touched with my fingertips. I lost myself this way, imagining, in a shimmer of strange and vibrant energy. I startled myself out of it, though, realizing who *was* in the room. I felt awful, as if I'd betrayed Richard in a terrible way. I drew the sheet around me even though it was hot, and shifted to the edge of the bed. Untouched, I lay awake, trying to figure this new thing out. When Richard woke up, I smiled sheepishly, and he knew something was up. He looked at me with his green-grey eyes, but I shrugged mine away, merely saying I had to go.

What was funny was that Richard seemed as captivated by the preacher as I was, not missing any opportunity to listen to him in the square. It was he who figured out his name was really Bienvenu. Welcome. Richard and I had coffee together in the cafe every day for the next week to hear him recite again and again the circumstances of the miracle.

He said the baby would be delivered out of his mouth, but he wasn't certain when, whether the period would be longer or shorter than the usual nine months for holy births. He believed it would be five months. He was trying to be careful of his burden but felt he could not really do harm, that the baby was protected from falls and bruises. Still, he said he did not understand how women did it, how they could be in the fields from sunup to sundown, thrashing, thrashing grain with babies in their bellies. And how they could go through the process eight or nine times. Truly, he said, woman is the closest we have on earth to the gods.

Sometimes people questioned him, asking him to expand on the significance of the birth. He answered in rhyme, from the freewheelin' years, from the electric era. Others were rude, not believing, wanting a fight, better still an arrest, but he was as Christian as could be and refused to become aroused. Most left him alone, for his prophecy was no longer news, and he was treated as a common street seer.

Then other rumors began, that he was not as pure as one might think, that he visited a brothel frequently, that he drank a bottle of rum toddy at night, that he smoked ganja. Of all the rumors only one was true: The preacher named Welcome liked to smoke marijuana now and then. When Richard lit up a joint and offered it to me, I, struck by a boldness inspired by the sun, offered it to the madman. He reached out his hand languidly and took the paper wet from my lips. Staring into my eyes, he took a deep drag and handed it back. He didn't hide the act, he didn't care if anyone watched. Richard was shocked that Be've'nu smoked.

"What's the big deal?" I asked, naming the saints and seers who used drugs to induce states of revelation. Even the Oracle at Delphi had been steeped in the fragrance of ganja. Drugs were not anathema to polytheistic religions; it was only the West that demanded that its clergy free their lives of the senses.

But think of the Buddhists, said Richard; they desire to be stone to temptation, to transcend the puerile pleasures of the earth, to meditate upon the godhead. And didn't Hindus require their mystics to go unadorned into the forests, relinquishing all worldly goods?

There's a difference between jewels and drugs, I said. Which is?, he asked.

To smoke is to ease out of the present, to get rid of the bonds of earth, to concentrate on the holy, I said, mad at him for being such a dolt.

But when a person is pregnant, the use of drugs . . . he said.

There was fire in the preacher's speech. It could move trees. His words whipped out from the dark to form illuminated pearls. He was so convinced of the truth of his beliefs that there was no room for anything else, and doubt shattered like glass around him. He was Orpheus, he was Apollo, he was Krishna who could swallow butter and reveal the world on his tongue. When the heat began to make blue spots appear before my eyes and turned the street into a river, I imagined the preacher was Bob Dylan in disguise, tanned and hidden, seeking refuge from the West. There's a wicked wind blowing from the upper deck, he said, and I searched vainly for the meaning of his words.

I saw him being bit by a dog. I saw him when dirty wash water landed at his feet. I saw him with his hand to his heart, feeling the life within him.

Never had the town been so hot. The preacher developed a habit of joining us at the cafe. He drank only water while Richard and I drained bottles of beer. Richard left us to get bottles of mineral water, which were on special.

The preacher and I did not speak to one another. He was seated on my right; droplets of heat appeared on his arm and face. His breath stirred my shirt. I was conscious of my breathing, my rising breasts. He smiled at me, right into the inside of me. It was so hot the air was rippling, the sounds around us amassed into one drone. He smiled into my eyes, his eyes were on my eyes, my mouth, my throat.

He held out his hand, and we walked toward a waterfall. We kept on brushing against one another, my fingers grazing his body, his hand near my shoulders, a whisper of contact. We sat under a tree. There was no one around us, nothing to interrupt us. His forehead was jeweled with sweat, and I lifted a large silk handkerchief to wipe his brow. His hair was bound up in bright string, and I untied it, letting it fall about his neck. The string turned to flowers, and roses were in his hair, in my hair.

O sister when I come to lie in your arms, do not treat me like a stranger, he said.

His words breathed into my ear.

You must realize the danger, he said.

His words roared like a lion as we embraced.

Time is like an ocean but it ends at the shore, he said.

His words whispered as he sank his teeth into my neck.

Richard came back. We were clothed and apart, seated and being served. I was shaking all over. A bus rattled down the road blowing exhaust. The sun traveled relentlessly in the sky.

The preacher Be've'nu left town the next day. The cafe owner said that he had delivered his message and was off to the next town. Some rumors floated about, of debts and robberies, but they were idle, played with to fan away the heat. I was sad and Richard could not help me.

Fourteen

"When you grow up, Richard, you'll never be stuck in rush hour." This is what Richard's mother had told Richard when he was young and living in New York. "When you become an artist, you'll sleep until eleven, and never face traffic," she said. Richard's mother was always talking like this, dreaming a future for her son that was miles away from her own experience as a design consultant at New Look Graphics, Inc. "Listen, I've been working since I was sixteen, mixing protein shakes and greens and juice for every Joe off the street. I studied at night and hustled like mad to make it. You don't need to do this." Constantly, Richard told me, she drummed into his head the benefits he'd have when he grew up.

Richard always spoke of his mother with irony, sometimes with genuine humor. His parents divorced when he was ten, and he'd lived with her in the "upper Eighties" in New York City, in an apartment that was primarily decorated in pink and white, with lots of plush couches and lots of plastic. She had already looked at an apartment for him in SoHo when he was attending high school, speculating incessantly about paint chips and fabric swatches. But Richard wanted to make documentaries and skipped college for Amsterdam. In a way, Richard's mother had groomed him for departure and travel to India all his life. I was five years old when he landed in Bombay in 1975.

She made commercial life seem awful but unwittingly made the life of an artist appear even worse. "I think she wanted me to paint so I could give her something to hang on her wall," he said, promising me he was joking.

I liked listening to Richard talk about his mother. It made him even more real in my life, giving him history, and for me, providing comedy. His upbringing sounded romantic to me, living in New York City, and then leaving. I made him recite the subway stops he'd use, and I'd chant with him—Lincoln Center, Columbus Circle, Times Square, Penn Station, Sheridan Square—because to me they sounded so magical. Tell me about the time you were in Washington Square and thought the "No Littering" sign was a long-lost friend, I'd say, or tell me about the time you skipped school and roamed about in Chelsea because that was the one place your mother's friends wouldn't be.

I also instinctively liked his mother. Here was some-one who cared deeply for her child and went to great lengths to provide for him. Interference, said Richard, but it seemed to me love. My mother wouldn't care what career I embarked upon after college, or where I lived. All she seemed to do was mock me, watch me like a curios-ity, if she could be bothered to see me at all. She was like the bird which abandoned her young in other birds' nests.

I knew something was up when I arrived at Richard's flat. A servant woman was doing his dishes, mopping up the floor, and he was picking up his discarded shirts from around the room. I liked the messiness of his life and was surprised at the busy cleaning.

"I don't believe it, but she's actually visiting," he said, staring at an unidentifiable stain on one of his T-shirts. "What do you think this is?" he asked.

"Who's coming?"

"Harriet."

"Your mother?"

"On holiday. With the Ladies Who Travel." Richard's mother belonged to a group of women who met monthly to travel to nearby places together. They liked to visit. Now the group was taking a "tour of the Orient," and his mother was to stay in India for a week, in Madras and Pondicherry. She then planned to spend an afternoon on Pi with Richard.

Richard hadn't seen his mother in five years. The last time they'd met was in London, when she'd sent him a ticket. "I was tripping, but not on purpose," he said. "It was pretty scary. I kept on thinking the salad was infinite."

He was nervous about my meeting her, but I looked forward to it.

She was arriving on Wednesday. I was impatient with my morning, trying on different outfits and trying to wear my hair up. Finally, I changed to what I had first put on and went over to Richard's flat. So it was with a sense of excitement that I met Richard's mother when she arrived on Pi.

Harriet was dressed in a purple and pink caftan, with earrings that looked like grape clusters and lots of bangles. Her hair was blond and worn up under a broad-brimmed hat. She was large and seemed a giant next to skinny Richard. I thought she was beautiful.

"This is my friend Sonil," he said.

She pressed her cheek to mine and kissed the air. I thought this only happened in the movies.

Then she announced that she might stay.

"Mom?"

"Baby, I understand why you want to live here. Life in America is worrisome. All that endless running and chatter. I'm ready for a change of pace. I want to be on a different level, mingle with real people, get in touch with myself."

"Mom, you're about ten years out of date."

"Is it too late to want spiritual fulfillment? Is it

wrong to add another dimension to my life? Are you telling me I'm too old, Richard?"

"You're not old. But living here—god, Mother, I don't think it's for you. And anyway, who would take care of the cats?"

"I can have them shipped here. They can become vegetarians. Stop worrying, Richard." She told us that she had already found a guru.

"I need to take a walk," said Richard, propelling me out of the door.

"What am I going to do? She can't possibly live here."

"She's your mother," I said.

"Exactly. Being on different continents suited me just fine. A guru! She'll probably organize Indo-Understanding weeks and Karma for Kleptomaniacs classes. You don't know my mother—she needs to control everything."

Richard's mother moved to the guru's camp. We decided to check the guru out. Her name was Helen Koenig. "My God, a goyishe guru," said Richard.

She was conducting a class on Dynamic Meditation.

"That's an oxymoron, isn't it?"

"You're getting hysterical."

"My mother is going to learn to meditate from a Nazi housewife from Duluth, and you think I'm getting hysterical?"

The Dynamic Meditation camp was located on six

acres that belonged to a former pilot. There were an assortment of buildings named "Earhart," "Lindy," and so on. We found a class being conducted at Wright House.

Helen Koenig was a compact woman in her forties, with cropped red hair, dressed in a chartreuse sweatsuit with an om symbol painted on the front. She was leading the class through a series of calisthenics to Muzak based on Leonard Cohen songs (who, it was rumored, had a summer home on the island).

"Empty your mind and let the energy flow in," she said as the group began to sway. Then the group began to hum.

"C'mon, people, don't hum, om," said Helen Koenig. "Droning doesn't get you anywhere. Break through your restraints."

The group consisted of about twenty people, mostly foreigners, with a stray Indian or two. Soon, they lay down in a circle and began to meditate. "No sleeping!" Helen would cry at intervals, "Meditate!" Finally, everyone got up and sang "With a Little Help from My Friends." Then they applauded and hugged one another.

"Isn't this wonderful?" gushed Richard's mom. "I feel so vitalized. I'm getting in touch with my energy centers." Richard just rolled his eyes.

We walked over to Markham House and entered the gift shop–cafe. Displays of quartzes, crystals on strings, rainbow stickers, ashram beads, tarot cards, T-shirts, and perfumed oils were neatly laid out on tabletops. A vaporizer streamed negative ions into the air, while soft sitar music drifted from high-tech speakers. Everything was expensive.

"The whole structure is wrong," said Richard, to me, or just to the air. Richard's mother told me about the different healing powers of crystals. She bought me a packet of stones to harmonize my inner child. We then joined Helen Koenig at the cafe. She had an oversized glass of wheat-grass juice in front of her. I ordered a tofu burger, and Richard selected a protein salad.

"Are you interested in Yoga?" she asked us. Richard told her he had studied it for years.

"An Indian instructor," he told her. I saw that he'd hurt Helen Koenig's feelings.

"We try to accommodate all forms of Eastern exercise, along with supervised diet. I've opened a series of Dynamic Meditation centers in California and Rhode Island and one in Washington, and they all use local produce and adopt their own regimen. Rhode Islanders like to swim, so they swim daily at their center."

I wondered what Rhode Island was as I tucked into the food. The tofu burger was quite good, warm and tasty, with much coriander chutney. They seemed to eat well. In fact, I enjoyed the atmosphere of this exercise and spirituality camp. And I was fascinated with Richard's mom, especially her clothes. The days passed. She wore a series of different-colored sweatsuits, with matching cloth caps and sneakers. Richard, however, seemed disconcerted by her appearance. "She used to wear business suits and clunky jewelry," he told me when Harriet went off to change into an aqua outfit. I couldn't tell which version of his mother he preferred.

I guess Richard believed that Pi was his territory, that his mother was trespassing. Somehow, her interest in spirituality was also a trespass, as if all sorts of lines were being crossed. I couldn't imagine my mother tracking me down if I went to the States. I couldn't understand Richard's embarrassment. Richard's mother was determined to stay on the island. "This is driving me crazy," he said to me.

"I think she's nice," I said.

"She is so . . . so . . ." As he struggled to find the word, I found my attention wandering. I had seen less of him before his mother's arrival, and I was beginning to think that I didn't know him well at all.

In fact, Richard had seemed very different to me for the past week or so. Still, I was unprepared when he spoke again.

"Sonil, I have to tell you something."

I'd already noticed that when people say they have to tell you something instead of just telling you, it's bound to be bad news.

"What?"

"I'm leaving for Ethiopia."

"What?"

"I can't stay here. The vibrations are all wrong. I think I can do better work there. I can't take this."

"What do you mean? What about your students? What about me?"

"I've got to get away."

"I think you're overreacting."

"I'll be back in August."

"But that's two months away!"

"Yeah, so it won't be long."

"Two months!" I cried. Didn't he realize how long that was? I might be gone before he returned.

"I might be gone before you return!"

"We can still be friends."

Fifteen

What was I to do with my Richardless days? I began to take walks, passionate nature hikes to untie myself from him. I pretended I was in a Jane Austen novel, but no Darcy appeared to quell my emotions. I wrote furious poetry. I took to sighting birds and noting them in a book. Saw: one parrot, rose-ringed, yellow-beaked. Saw: three ravens, nearly big as sheep. Saw: a bunch of seagulls, an air full of sparrows.

"I got his note, yes," said Richard's mother, munching on a carrot. She ushered me into her dormitory.

"We are both of us restless spirits. When Richard moved to India, I decided to move to California. I said goodbye to all my New York friends, who thought I was crazy, and sold most of my things. I tied a trailer to the back of an old car and rode westward like a pioneer. In California, I was introduced to the suburbs. Bicycles scattered over the lawns. The paper delivered daily by a boy saving up for a deluxe skateboard, maybe college. Garbage collected twice a week, not to mention curbside recycling. I bought a house, got cable, settled in. But before that, I stopped in Kansas City for a week.

"In Kansas City I had met a man, a farmer. He sold flowering shrubs at a very fair price and lived off his soybean produce. His father had been a farmer and his father before him. He had a history that my husband didn't have, that I barely had. He was uglier than my husband, but I liked him more for it. But he was married, and I was divorced and on my way to California. My last night there he took me to a dance hall in a town called River and slow-danced with me. That was the most intimate we ever got. Seven years later his wife died, and he wrote to me. But I had moved on."

Richard's mother paused, not looking at me anymore.

"But you could go back," I said. Richard's mother just smiled and looked wistful.

"Young love is difficult," she said.

This family spoke in puzzles and was destined for sadness, I thought.

I was going to Radcliffe, by God. I was going to become a zoologist. And if the admissions personnel were to inquire if I ever had any other loves besides animals, I would resolutely say "No." There would be no Richard in my life. But I was afraid they would somehow know I had had a lover. They would deny me entrance. I would be stuck in Madras. No one would ever marry me, not because of my mother's reputation, but because somehow my love for Richard would be found out.

I told Maria that Richard had left. She hugged me fiercely, and I had a feeling she already knew. I began to sob on her shoulder, great sobs for myself. Why did he have to go away? Why did he leave me? What had I done? Maria soothed me but she could not help me. When I had worn myself of tears, she made us some tea and spoke of Richard.

"He had a roommate in college who was Indian, did he ever tell you that? This Indian boy would make paranthas and dahl and fed the two of them all winter. He told Richard stories about Cochin, his sister who was the beauty in the family, his two older brothers who were indifferent and glum. That was how India wove its spell over him."

"India doesn't weave spells," I said, indignantly. "It's the West that's the spell-weaver, the enchanter, enticing us with Coca-Cola and television."

"Well, maybe all nations are magicians. Maybe the media are magicians. But whatever it was, Richard began to dream of India. He thought it would cure him of his terrible disappointment with life. I think he found in you an extension of his dreams, India as a young girl, India as innocence, intelligence, and wit. And I think when his mother came here, he saw that he didn't have solitary possession of India, that his mother sought claim on his fantasy. So he left. I think his leaving is irresponsible. Remember he is leaving his mother as well as you. He has not yet grown up."

But even as she spoke thus, I began to think of his eyes and his hair and all the things I loved about him and his special tenderness toward me. I heard what Maria said but my thoughts were too distracted. I thought of his voice and his breath and the smell of his clothes, and I felt I could die right then and there. I had had something so beautiful in him. But then I guessed that I was succumbing to obsession, and it was all his fault. And my mother's fault—for wasn't it she from whom I'd inherited this passion? I had become as wanton as she was. I started to cry again, and Maria handed me a handkerchief and hugged me again.

I went to the temple thinking that perhaps Jani was on the right track, that perhaps religion was the answer for a disquieted mind. There was a group who sat next to me on the bus that also got off when I did, and it turned out that they, too, were going to the temple. The temple in our town was a famous one, built in A.D. 325. It featured a highly refined sculptural base depicting the entire story of the Ramayana and a legion of gods and goddesses on the remaining facades. I washed my hands at the tap and removed my sandals and went in. My group consisted of a widowed grandmother, her daughter or daughter-in-law, who had an infant in her arms, and two chattering ten-year-old girls. I applied a red dot to my forehead at the entrance.

What I best liked about this temple was the host of smells emanating from every corner. It was a mixture of incense oil, stone, and something else which I can only describe as godly presence. It was bewitching and always swept me into my better nature. I became more thoughtful, more full, somehow, tranquil and expansive. My group was doing a special puja, and I watched as they gave coconuts and bananas and flowers to the priest. He placed their offerings at the feet of the principal figure, praying aloud in Sanskrit and tearing up the flowers to scatter at the feet of the lesser deities. Then the camphor lamp was passed around, and I touched its warmth and then my eyes. The priest gave me a yellow chrysanthemum and handed my group their coconuts and fruit, now blessed.

This temple featured a small shrine for Sita, an avatar of Laxshmi; here she was depicted as a thoughtful companion to Rama, wife of the avatar of Vishnu and hero of the epic. Sita followed her husband into the forest for fourteen years of exile and was abducted by the evil Ravana. Captive in his garden, but untouched because she was a goddess, she awaited rescue. When Rama finally reclaimed her as well as his kingdom, the people muttered that Sita was impure, having been separated from her husband and living in another man's home. Required to take a test for purity, Sita walked through fire. But once her innocence was proved, her eyes blazed with anger at the injustice done to her, and she returned to the earth from which she'd sprung, leaving Rama.

I stood before the shrine to pray. I prayed for my grandmother's good health, and Jani's, and I prayed for the welfare of my cousins and my aunts. Finally, I asked the goddess for extra strength to see my mother as she truly was and to help me get over Richard's absence. I prayed for forgiveness from the goddess, and I asked for a boon: to make my judgment clearer. I bowed before the goddess and then took a walk all around the temple.

I met my group as they collected their sandals. The girls were giggling, and the mother looked annoyed and the grandmother impatient. They went to a vendor and got sugarcane to munch on. I felt thirsty and unthinkingly drank from the tap. I was not ever to drink outside water, but I had forgotten. Immediately I wondered if I'd get sick, and I said an extra prayer to let this not come to pass.

I fed a banana to the elephant outside and took the bus home.

. . .

"What, my girl, you've been to the temple without anyone knowing?" asked my astonished grandmother. I nodded, feeling tired and a bit dizzy.

"I'm hungry. Can I have lunch?"

"We've eaten. I'll get the cook to get you something.
My God, this child went to the temple by herself! Come
here! What were you thinking of?"

My grandmother hugged me to her bosom, and I
breathed in the odor of her sari and her comfortable
presence. She fetched me a plate of rotis and sweet
potato. I ate quickly and still felt faintly ill.

I remembered the water from the tap but couldn't
begin to tell my grandmother anything.

The next day I awoke crying. I had lost Richard, I
had no mother to speak of, and I had probably caught
hepatitis from the temple tap water. I got up, sneaked
out, and took the bus to see Maria again. On the way, a
man with a sad face stared at me and moved next to my
seat. My inner antennae went up like an ant's that senses
something amiss, while my mind told me not to be para-
noid. The man began to mumble and leaned against me.
I shoved him aside and found another seat. In panic, I
wondered if because I had slept with Richard it meant
that I was now sending a signal to random males that I
was available for anything. The man continued to press
against me in my mind, and I despaired at being female,

at being on a bus, and of making love long before I was old enough to appreciate the consequences.

"Sonil," said Maria when I was seated on her sofa, "we search for love all our lives just as we search for family all the time. And whenever we take on anyone as a friend, we also take on their families and their history. This does not have to be a bad thing. It broadens our sense of self. Letting Richard into your life was not a sin. In fact, nothing is good or bad, and we don't really need to judge at all . . ."

Again I drifted off and looked at her bungalow. It seemed nice, with its heavy brocade drapes and trailing plants hung from the ceiling. The light was good and her furniture, dark mahogany, Raj style, looked settled. I liked her cushions made from pallus, the richly embroidered borders of saris. Maybe someday if I had my own apartment, I could live well and have people to visit. Maybe I could keep a lover or keep a dog. I wondered if I would need a lot of money for such a life

". . . In America, if you have a heartbreak you can tap into a network of female sympathizers, women who will listen to your problems about men and offer solutions. Even girls your age discuss such things. There are magazines that cater to this sort of trouble, with questions and answers about boyfriend problems, quizzes on compatibility. It's quite an industry. Indian girls must talk about these things, too."

I supposed girls my age rhapsodized over film stars or a cricket player, occasionally a cousin or a brother's friend. But marriage at a suitable age was always the target, always an aim, an outcome that restricted behavior somewhat. Of course, there were stories of girls sneaking off from college to meet their beaus, kissing at train stations, but the large majority of my classmates would acquiesce to arranged marriages and start families within three years of the wedding.

But what if no one ever loved me again, or if I never loved anyone again? Would I be as unlucky in love as my mother? I felt doomed.

"I wouldn't worry about all those things, Sonil. I would forgive myself for being in love with Richard and move on. You have so much life ahead of you, my God, so much to explore and accomplish."

But I couldn't see past Richard. I desperately wanted him next to me, immediately, always. I said goodbye to Maria and turned toward home, but then changed my mind and went into a cafe.

I thought about animals and their capacity for change, how species evolved one after another, left and right, front and back. I thought about continual reproduction, and what that meant in terms of survival. And I began to think of the ability to abstain from love as a peculiarly human trait. But then, that couldn't be true, I thought; surely there were earthworms that were monkish in their habits?

. . .

Why didn't I abstain? Why didn't my mother? Why could she not follow the proper path of widowhood? Why couldn't she remain content with who she was? What was so bad in being a proper widow? "A widow is nothing in our society. Unable to remarry, unable to entertain, always an eyesore, a begrudged extra plate," one of my teachers had lectured in class. But was that always the case? Why did she need to entertain anyway?

Now, knowing Richard, I saw how sweet it was to lie with someone. Still, could she not hold off? Of course, I wouldn't have been born if she had held off, if she had remained satisfied with her life. I think dissatisfaction makes us impatient with the slow pace of natural progression, propels us forward. Of course, this dissatisfaction could be good . . . Survival might depend upon it. But maybe it would have been better if I hadn't been born.

"Hey, professor, what are you thinking?"

It must be my fate to be accosted in cafes. I looked up. It was C.P.'s cousin who liked cricket.

"Nothing," I said. "How are you?"

"I just finished a game. The boys here are not bad."

"I'm sorry about C.P.," I said, immediately wishing I hadn't.

"Did she really go off to a convent?" he said, admiringly.

I nodded.

"Wow."

"Yes."

"What are you studying?"

"First year P.U.C."

"I'm in eleventh standard."

We had run out of conversation, I thought, but Murthi, C.P.'s cousin, began to talk of a movie he had seen, which made me say that I wanted to see it, too. He said his sister was going with her friends and did I want to go; he could ask her to ring me? And to all this I answered yes, why not? I gulped my milk and thought, To hell with Richard.

The movie was a good one, a regular weepy epic with lots of drama, two heroines and two heroes, five villains, all taking place near a temple and a hill station in India. A Hindi film with good songs, and when the front row audience began to sing along, Murthi's sister and her friends began to giggle and I giggled, too. But in the second half, the hero reminded me of Richard, and I cried and hoped no one noticed. I began to wish I had never met Richard, that I was still an innocent girl, like the girls around me who were shy about certain subjects.

After the movie we went out for espresso and ice cream, and the girls discussed the film and their friends. They didn't pay too much attention to me, so I was left to dream on.

I began to fashion a Richard from my memory of him. In my inner world he was even more attentive, more alluring than he had been in reality. He had been gone two weeks. I dreamed up long conversations with him, scenarios in which I spoke my own mind clearly and at length. He replied with utter devotion, a multitude of compliments. For a while I waited to receive a letter from him, but none arrived. I reasoned that he might have thought it dangerous to send mail to me at my grandmother's, that it would arouse suspicious attention.

"Why don't you begin a project—some drawing?" asked my grandmother.

I said no, I didn't want to draw.

"Do a painting for me," she sweetly suggested.

I had drawn those mandalas for her but she never knew. I decided to attempt some painting, but my paints looked dull. Great-uncle had some better colors, and dispiritedly I borrowed his and sat down to paint.

I tried some images of girls, having learned from one of my classmates how to draw a quick portrait. I had small squares of paper, also borrowed from Great-uncle. Idly, then more seriously, I began to draw some portraits of Richard. I drew his broad forehead, his strong nose, his quick smile. I drew from a memory that seemed to have been burned into my mind. As I drew I felt myself ache with longing. I forgot the verandah, the birds, the house, Grandmother. I had completely entered the world of my dreams, where time stood utterly still. I was with Richard in my mind. It was almost like dying and entering another dimension. But somehow I snapped myself out of this trance and was conscious that I had lost minutes. I was surprised to see the sun high in the sky and to hear my grandmother calling me to lunch.

Meanwhile, my mother began to disappear in the evenings, too. Usually, she ate her meals alone on the verandah. After my supper, Grandmother would set her a plate of food. Sometimes my mother would take her plate to the garden, where she surreptitiously sipped wine. But for a few nights, she missed her evening meal; late at night I'd hear the garden gate creaking open and my mother entering the compound. I began to notice that she disappeared on Tuesdays, Thursdays, and Saturdays. Sometimes she came home laden with lilac. Blooms of wet purple were cradled in her arms, and a strange smile floated on her lips. I knew then she had gone to visit her friend the poet.

The poet lived a few blocks from us. She was a woman in her forties who was famous for her female lovers. Her books of poems were dedicated to them. To Kavita with Love. To Lalitha with Devotion. To Radha, My Happiness. She produced dozens of these slender volumes, hand-printed by our local press. My mother was not a lover, as far as I knew, and no poems had been dedicated to her. But she and the poet had been friends a long time; I think they went to school together.

I imagined the two of them in early evening, on deeply pillowed couches, sitting in Sapphic splendor, sipping tea. Maybe they traded romantic anecdotes, revealed secret conquests. Maybe they braided each other's hair and massaged each other's backs. I supposed they read poetry to each other. My mother always came back peaceful and dreamy, and holding flowers from the poet's garden.

But where did my mother go when she returned with no flowers? Where else did my mother go? There were places she roamed that I had no idea of. Sometimes she was gone for hours, sometimes for an entire night. Maybe she had trysts in the city. Maybe she met a handsome playboy, a man who drove her around in a spotless white car, who would take her out to a meal at a five-star hotel. She might be dressed in her finest, her mouth lipsticked and bright, her lids heavy with shadow. Or maybe she lounged in the arms of a vegetable seller, the two of them drunk on rum, sprawled on a sidewalk. But this was harder for me to imagine. I could not see her with a man without money, only with someone who would make her forget herself for a while. But, and this might have been closest to the truth, I thought she was usually alone. She was brave enough to walk anywhere she pleased. I could see her drinking alone under the stars, waiting for the pink tinge of dawn to usher her home.

In this town, my mother was granted special status that let her walk unpestered through the streets. No one flicked a greeting her way; no one invited her to talk about the weather or someone's baby. They denied her the closeness of people tied up in bystander talk, the contact of eyes, perhaps a brush of fingertips on the arm, a good-natured laugh that unites us with our fellow men well within the strictures of propriety, a bond that promises nothing and demands even less. Sharing a few words about the rain doesn't oblige anyone to issue dinner invitations.

But rapists could still get to my mother. They could grab her breasts in the darkness, knee her apart, tear off her sari. Hoodlums could take their pleasure with my mother, although I was certain that they were afraid of her. She would claw at their eyes, she would curse their lives, she'd kick their groins hard. My mother was nothing if not tough.

At night, I asked my grandmother to tell me stories. She told me the story of the Pole Star. She said that there was once a king who had two wives. The first wife bore him a son of whom he was very fond, but the second wife was very jealous. She persuaded the king to banish the first wife and son from the kingdom, and so much under the power of the second wife was he that he complied with the request. The first wife and her son lived in a hut at the edge of a great forest. When the child was seven years old, he asked his mother to tell him who his father was. When she did, he asked her where his father dwelt. When she told him, the son wished to visit his father and set off. The king was delighted to see his son again and embraced him many times. But the minute his second wife entered the hall, he hastily set down his son. The son was so hurt by this that he quietly crept away from the palace and went home.

At home, he asked his mother if there was anyone stronger than his father.

Yes, replied his mother, it is the Lotus-Eyed.

And where does the Lotus-Eyed dwell, Mother?

She told her son that the Lotus-Eyed lived in the heart of the forest, surrounded by tigers and bears, hoping to discourage her son from seeking him out. But that night, the son arose and kissed his mother softly goodbye. He walked through the forest, not knowing whom he was seeking but knowing his name. So simple was his desire and so innocent, that he had no fear in him. He did not expect that anything could harm him.

In the forest he met a tiger and asked, Are you the Lotus-Eyed? The tiger said no. He met a bear and asked, Are you the Lotus-Eyed? The bear said no.

Finally a sage came by (and, you know, this was God himself) and said, "To find the Lotus-Eyed, you must chant his name aloud."

And so the boy chanted. And by chanting, he discovered God within himself, as well as the knowledge that he contained his father. He became the Pole Star, and he now guides others on their travels and their quests.

My grandmother stopped speaking. The sky had filled with stars, and I felt as if I'd never seen them before, so bright were they. I held my grandmother's hand and together we waited for my mother's return. We both fell asleep.

Sixteen

My mother returned at dawn. She said nothing to my grandmother and me. She walked past us. Later I heard my grandmother scolding my mother with exasperation and concern. But my mother's replies were muffled. I ate my breakfast and listened to the radio. Later, I sneaked into my mother's room and stole some of her poetry books. I thought I might find out something about my mother by reading her friend's verse. I kept on telling myself that she deserved to have such treatment from me if she refused to address my needs. Guiltily, I looked at the books. They were beautiful, worn and weighty when I placed one between my palms. The lettering was embossed, and some of the gilt was worn.

There was no picture of the poet on the back of her books. I imagined her with wild, unruly hair, a faraway expression in her eyes. I wondered what it would be like to kiss a woman. Soft, I guessed, feather-light. I kissed my arms to see if I could tell, but I knew it couldn't be the same. Maybe women were better off with women; they were more alike. I opened my mouth and kissed my hand slowly and sensually, imagining the poet's mouth on mine. It made me shiver.

I began to read. Her poems began simply, strings of images attached with threads of herbs, fragrant jasmine, lush rose. Then this string was stretched taut, and the herbs gave way to polished stones. Pain and conflict skidded on the surface, dug deep like needles piercing, drew blood, tears. Lovers were listed, cast off, abandoned, cheated on.

> *My eyes are full of your jet-black hair*
> *It chokes my dreams and your sweet tongue releases berry*
> *   juice in my mouth*
> *I aim for the milk in you*
> *Stars scatter at your footstep*
> *The moon loses itself in your skin.*

She spoke of anger, betrayal, and whispered apologies.

> *When Krishna fled from Radha, she turned to her own*
> *   playmates for comfort*
> *What could the blue-skinned god give in place of the soft*
> *   hands of her friends as they undressed her?*

I stopped reading. I stretched and sensed the world as if through a fog, yet aware of my own movements. Everything seemed peaceful, dreamy. I had read some poems and felt good. They hadn't told me that she liked poetry. I walked out of my room, which suddenly seemed cleaner and better than before. I felt like I could kiss everyone. Richard was away; let him be, I thought, maybe he will discover something worthwhile. Meanwhile, I had a day at my disposal. No wandering around town aimlessly, no need to rush urgently to his apartment, seeking his arms. No need to wish violently for something that wasn't mine to have.

But what to do? No one was at home. Grandmother was visiting a friend with whom she played Parcheesi. I decided to apply polish to my toenails, which occupied me for half an hour. Then I called up C.P.'s cousin and asked him if he wanted to visit. He agreed and brought over a book for me to read. We spent the afternoon talking about school and the movies and told stupid jokes without exhaustion. We went for a bike ride, and then he left and I fixed myself a snack and waited for my grandmother's return. It seems all I did was wait for someone else that summer.

Then idly I wondered if Richard had found someone in Africa. A dark Ethiopian beauty. How old would she be, I wondered, suddenly bitter, angry, choking on my imagination. Would he caress her as he had done me and all the others before me? Would he make pancakes afterward? I tried to concentrate on something else, nearly crying from the strain of it, but even if I just chanted zoology, a litany of what I had memorized out of a textbook, Richard came up all over again. He was a distraction, an error, a wrong turn, and *why* did he leave me? Was it my color? My age? The impossibility of loving an Indian island girl with a horrible family? Instantly I was ashamed—not horrible, merely eccentric, odd. Was he embarrassed by me? Was he ashamed of me, in the final analysis, in the distant and full picture? I wept all night against my pillow after the lights were off.

He had left because of his mother. That much was clear. But in his absence I began to think and therefore undermined myself. Would he come back to me? Was I worth coming back for? More to the point, was he worthy of me, headed for Radcliffe and my own job in Africa? How dare he go to Ethiopia before me? It was my dream he had supplanted. *I* wanted to see the Transvaal, the Serengeti. Deep deserts and indomitable plains. Rushes of sunset in the sky, rhinos outlined against the horizon. And giraffes. And leopards and gazelles, swift-footed and tame. If I was a gazelle, what was Richard? A lion? Or merely a man whom I missed to distraction?

The next day my grandmother took me to the bank. Ahead of us in the queue was an American man with his young son. Watching him I was struck with an understanding that had escaped me most of my previous life.

Watching this stranger, this American father, his hands in his pockets, his feet shod in sneakers, as I stood in line with my grandmother, I looked at the larger picture. My grandmother, who only meant kindness, asked for the third time if I did not wish to use the rest room, which filled me with humiliation—as if I were five! As if I didn't understand my body. Instead of thinking of something else to say, I could only wish to be someone else. There stood the American, confident and knowing, his watch sparkling, his shoes scuffed.

I realized that I could never have that, that American symbiosis with the world, the ease of knowing that if life was indeed a river, he was part of it, not helpless, not alien, but part of it. It was something I could never have, no matter how hard I tried; I would never be able to cut myself loose from my family. It was my aunts, my uncles, my great-uncle, my grandmother, all of them in their noisy, quarrelsome ways, their pettiness, their awkwardness, that would burst out of my seams, no matter what my affectations.

My mother tried to escape it. She tried to dress differently, to use her beauty to make up for not being white or rich or cultured, to use her sexuality to make up for having the natural self-consciousness of our family. And as for me with Richard, I saw not only the man, but more: I saw ease, something that had to do with eating hot dogs, with sports, with the strength to lift a hammer as well as throw a Frisbee, with animal casualness, with

American confidence. He was everything that no one in my family was; it was everything I wanted to be. But simple association wasn't enough. Even if I were smarter and prettier than an American girl, even with my youth, it would be the American girl who would be welcomed into Richard's relatives' houses, it would be she whom they'd understand. Even if we were to be married, I'd never gain admittance into his extended family, his family who were tied to memories of Thanksgiving dinners, backyard baseball, first dates and first cars, roots that I didn't have. Being half American wasn't enough. I remembered the Joyce story "Araby," where the narrator suddenly realized some truth about himself and sees himself for a vain and horrible creature; I recognized the vanity in myself thus, standing in line.

But my grandmother did a surprising thing. She clicked open her handbag, and taking out her sunglasses, she gave them to me. I was forced to regard her. "These are for you. They are to chase foolish thoughts away from your head," she said. I inspected the gift. They were Ray-Bans from abroad, from London or America, maybe Australia. I tried them on, and although they were loose about my head, I saw things differently through them. The American noticed me and smiled, and I, despite my alienation, smiled back. My family had triumphed again.

Seventeen

Still. I sighed to the trees and sighed over the grass and sighed over the gate of our house. I felt rejected and dejected, far away from the comfort of anyone I knew. At this time, I began to ride the bus. I would buy a ticket and ride round-trip without getting off at any stop. I'd wait for the bus to start its journey again. I lost interest in everything at home, even my mother.

My great-uncle returned from wherever it was he'd gone, and entreated me to play cards or join him and my grandmother in Parcheesi. We called it "Dayakatum." I would quit before the game concluded. I began to practice distracted Yoga and uneven Tai Chi Chuan. I continued reading the poetry I found in my mother's room. When I tried to sleep, I couldn't.

One night, I took my sleeplessness to the verandah.

I peered into the darkness, not sure what I wanted to see, aside from Richard striding across the courtyard coming back to me. Perhaps it was my state of mind, or the shadows of the trees made by the watchlight. I thought I saw my mother in the arms of a ghost. I saw her embrace a shadow. Was it my father? I looked closer. Was he wearing a cowboy hat? I watched my mother in her sari twirl around with this stranger in her arms, watched them execute steps like Nargis and Raj Kapoor, movie stars in motion. The ghost held her close, his arm about her waist, the other holding my mother's arm. Her sari glittered white, and were it not for the fact that they hovered in midair, I might have been seeing something real. I became afraid. I felt out of control. A dread seized me, sucking out my breath so that I gasped. A convulsion gripped my heart. I drew away and remained awake the rest of the night. In desperation, I wrote to Jani.

Dear Jani,

What I am about to tell you will probably shock you, but I feel you must know. I think I saw a ghost. It was a vision of my mother. Also I have known a man here who is actually quite old and is more than a friend. When you left I began to see him more and more, and now he has left the island and I do not know what I can do about it. I know it was wrong of me, but he was like a beckoning Krishna, and like any gopika, I danced toward him. Don't laugh at

me, Jani. Now he has left, and I am inconsolable and see-
ing things. What shall I do?

Your loving cousin,
Sonil

When dawn came through my window, I sealed the letter and searched for a stamp. I went to the kitchen for a cup of coffee, and found Vasanti muttering in the kitchen. My mother had been found drunk on the front steps that morning, and Vasanti had had to bring her in.

"What did her sandals look like?" I asked.

Vasanti threw me a distracted glance.

I remembered the story of the Dancing Princesses who would steal away each night to visit their dream lovers, their worn-out shoes the only clue to their disappearance. Leaving Vasanti, I went to the foyer to check on the sandals, but I couldn't find her pair. My grandmother was watering the lawn, and something about the line of her mouth kept me from asking any questions. I spent the day inside, idly reading, thinking of Richard now and then. I looked at more poems by the poet.

Three days later I received this letter from Jani:

My dear Sonil,

I admit your news was a bit surprising, but do not despair. Young love is powerful, but it is just that: young. Perhaps you were also taken advantage of, in your innocence and inexperience. But your heart is very strong, and soon you will be able to put this business behind you.

I assume that there were no lingering attachments on his part. I think it very advisable to come visit me for a month or two weeks. You will be able to relax and get away from the town, and after that, you will be headed back to school. I am sure our grandmother will like this idea. Why not ask her and then write to me immediately?

Yours always,
Jani

I was very happy at the offer. It seemed the best thing to do. Going away might help me regain my balance. But when I asked my grandmother, she said no. Why ever not, I demanded. And then my grandmother said that my mother would miss me.

"But she doesn't even care about me!" I said.

"Nevertheless, you are her daughter, and you cannot leave when any minute things might change."

"What things?" I demanded.

My grandmother was cryptic and refused to say any more. But I persisted.

"When you were born, you were as tiny as a teacup. We were so afraid you wouldn't live. I said prayers daily, and Mrs. Narayan walked to the temple for us every day, as well. You wouldn't accept milk, so we had to feed you with formula through an eye dropper. Slowly you gained strength and weight. You no longer felt like a dry leaf in my arms."

"Did you hold me a lot?"

"I could hardly bear to put you down."

"And my mother?"

"She suffered a great deal. The loss of your father was a hard blow. I think you inherited his mouth, because she could not look at you without crying."

"So she avoided me."

"Not like that. But it was too much for her, and we decided to send you to Shalani and Leila as soon as you were old enough."

"So she could have her affairs in private."

"Sonil—it may be hard for you to understand, but your mother did her best for you."

"So why did she neglect me? Why does she get drunk at night and meet strange men? Why does she disgrace us?"

"I don't think she meets men. I think most men are probably afraid of her. She is strong in her own right—the only thing that she is afraid of possibly is you."

"Afraid of me?"

"You have so much anger toward her. You must learn to be more generous."

I stared past my grandmother.

I missed Jani and after watching me mope for three days, my grandmother relented and off I went.

The travel by rail was fun in that I was setting off for a part of Pi that I had never seen. The convent was fifty miles away to the east, in a sleepy town. I sat next to a man who was a singer from California, who told me that he was also a Buddhist monk. He was delighted that I was going to the Sacred Heart Convent because he thought it a very good sort of place. He said he came to Shankar Nagar three months every year just to meditate, which, considering his very busy schedule, was impressive. He showed me his computerized date book, and I saw that he had events planned as far as five years ahead.

We both got off at the same station, and he steered me toward the convent. The convent was a white building enclosed by a wall with a garden in front of it. Several nuns were pulling out carrots and gathering them in a large basket. In my pocket I had the name of the Californian, the monk whose latest recording was a series of devotional prayers set to wind chimes. I planned to purchase the disk when I went back to Madras. He bid me a cheery farewell, and off I went to seek my cousin.

Finding her was not a problem. I asked the gardening nuns, and they pointed me toward the gate. As I walked toward it, a bell began to ring, announcing that it was two in the afternoon. The gate was ajar, and I wandered in. To my surprise, I found a very nice house with a verandah where a group of nuns was sitting around a girl who was playing a guitar. It was so bucolic, so serene, I just stared for a long while. Then, becoming self-conscious, I walked past them, uncertain as to whether to interrupt them and ask where Jani was or just to go into the house. I decided to go into the house. The nuns listening to the strumming smiled benignly and began to sing. I started to giggle; I mean, it was rather funny, singing nuns in a cloister, and me, a young girl who didn't know where she was going. Luckily, I noticed a pump gurgling with water, and realizing I was thirsty, I seized the moment to take a drink.

The water was cold, and it cleared my head of silliness. Inside, there was a waiting area and a large notebook for visitors. There was a bell that one could ring for assistance, and ring it I did.

"May I help you?" asked a woman who seemed to materialize suddenly.

"I am looking for Janaki Visnuwath," I told her.

I met Jani in the back, hanging her wash on a line in the courtyard. She smiled as I ploughed into her arms.

"I know three things," she told me. "Poetry can move your heart. Solitude can grant you wisdom. And love comes from a peaceful mind.

"Let me write it down for you," she laughed, as she saw my moody mouth pointing downward.

"Isn't love about passion?"

"I wouldn't know," said Jani. She looked past me, seeing something I couldn't see. Jani was like Joan of Arc, I thought. I never had to save her with a sword. She had worn one all along.

I was given a cot in a room for visitors. I slept under a photograph of Mother Teresa. I awoke early, took a bath at a communal shower, having walked down three flights of stairs clutching my towel and soap. I joined the other nuns for a simple but filling breakfast (idlis, juice, beans-curry) and then either followed Jani as she did her chores or read while she prayed. Nearly every day we went for a long walk, and when we couldn't because of rain, we stayed in and helped make chapatis. Jani helped out at a class teaching calisthenics, and I exercised alongside the schoolchildren, stretching up and down. These children were orphans whom the convent supported with help from the government. I talked with Jani most when she did laundry.

I asked her how it was she chose to be a believer in Christ, and if that meant she had to be solitary.

"I mean, you haven't even given love a chance."

"But my Lord tells me to have only love in my heart."

"I meant boys, Jani."

"I would rather remain single, give my life in the service of God. This way I can help others while helping myself."

"But what about kissing?" I asked. "Aren't you curious about it?"

She looked at me with amusement, which I must confess infuriated me. How could Jani know that sex and marriage were not for her?

"Sonil, once I was in love with someone in Delhi. Her family moved to Bombay, and she never answered my letters. Later, I found out that she had died. I went to the tiny garden Auntie Roja has and wondered what to do. As I was thinking, I saw an angel, who came toward me and smiled. I was filled with such light, such happiness. This is how I began to believe in God. Even more than mortal man."

"Can't you also love God and man—woman—at the same time?"

"No, I cannot."

She said it with such sad certainty, I wondered if she wasn't being a martyr, suffering silently. Then again, given my own unhappiness, maybe she had stumbled upon a truth, and love in God provided her with a barrier from the world of mortals.

"But in fact," said Jani, reading my mind, "I am not hiding myself from the world. We teach children, go to the market, and sometimes even go on holiday to the seashore. We aren't locking ourselves in the convent all day and night. But a certain amount of solitude is necessary for contemplation and peace of mind. We then become stronger to help others."

She was convinced of her words, but I wasn't. She was missing out, I knew that much for certain. And this girl in Bombay, that sounded like something from a story. I doubted there was a girl, only fear. But if a person is truly fearful, then one has to placate one's fears and do whatever is possible to cure that timidity. Jani did not look fearful; she looked calm, collected, steady in her thoughts. Whatever made her a nun was whatever made her who she was from the start.

And again I began to wonder if I shouldn't have followed in her footsteps, become a devotee of God. Perhaps then I wouldn't have suffered over Richard. I could have preserved my honor as well as my pride. But there was Radcliffe and all my plans. Maybe that was selfish, too, the desire to go overseas and become a great scientist. A great anything smacked of hubris, and I became very doubtful. Everything one could want in life I had: air, food, shelter, strength. But then I had found an even greater contentedness, at a cafe with a man whom I loved. Maybe it was the wanting that led people astray. Maybe it was like acquisition; one always strives for more. If happiness, then more happiness. Didn't Madonna have a song about this? I decided to give the matter no further thought.

"I don't think it's wrong to love a girl when you are a girl. One thing the nuns might disagree with, but still. I loved Asha, I was infatuated, I strove to be like her. And she loved me. Maybe if she'd lived, we could have lived together, and I could have borne the world better. But God called her, and at the same time He called me."

I listened to Jani, idly playing with a piece of grass. Loving girls, she couldn't love boys. Loving Asha, she couldn't love C.P. I drew the blade across my knee, liking the tickling, then suddenly feeling self-conscious as I remembered kissing myself. I wanted to kiss Jani, pull her toward me, make her leave the convent. Who needed boys anyway? But Richard was too strong, too present, too new. Jani looked eternally sad. Asha and Richard. They had kissed us and marked us and left us. They had conquered and retreated and declared checkmate.

There was a pond at the convent. During early evening prayers, I slipped off my clothes and slid into the water. It was delicious, enveloping. I bobbed up and down for a while and then ducked down to open my eyes. The interior was murky, greenish. My eyes smarted, and I surfaced. Dragonflies landed near me and buzzed overhead. Silvery fish darted away. I floated on my back, exposed and not caring. No one could see. I thought about Krishna and the gopis, how he had spied on them, laughing at their nakedness. How embarrassed they had been upon discovery, how quick their hands flew to cover themselves. But surely there had been one gopi who didn't care, who didn't blush and hide but floated like this to let the god appraise her, whose breasts rose like flowers from the water, whose hair glinted like a mermaid's. A maid who challenged the god to look as he might, to understand that her body was hers alone, even if he possessed it, to know that her bathing was an act of self. And I couldn't help thinking that Krishna withdrew his eyes and turned to the others, who were flustered, who were angered, and that he let the brave girl alone. He didn't dance with her or clasp his leg around her or cover her with blue-lipped caresses. The girl had met his boldness with her own and somehow proved a point. A girl who might have strolled like my mother out of the water without shame, let her body dry in the sun, and chosen any lover who pleased her. And perhaps her love was another girl, a creature she could mock and adore at the same time, whose hair she could plait, whose ears she could fill with song, knowing she had defeated Krishna himself. But her first kiss would be for the god who let her alone, who withdrew his eyes. And as she lay with her lovers, maybe she realized that she was equal to the peacock-feathered, blue-skinned flute player. But the poets never wrote about this.

I finished my swim and went back to the nuns.

After ten days at the convent, we received a phone call. I took it, expecting a scolding from my grandmother about the sweater I'd left behind. Instead it was my mother on the phone. My grandmother had died.

Eighteen

Arriving at Madhupur for the funeral was oddly easy; suddenly all the trains were available and on time. Jani and I traveled together, of course, and there were at once so many helpful people to carry her luggage and the food we packed. No one seemed to notice that we were unusually quiet and in a state of shock, because when we got the news, we acted normally, as if we were just making the trip back as scheduled.

My grandmother. My green hill. O, my grandmother, how could this happen? It must not have happened. If only I could do something to reverse it all. My grandmother. My grandmother, my dear, darling, lovely, brave, practical, doting grandmother. My eyes filled with tears, my nose started to run, my chest began to panic. My body began to heave, although with a supreme effort, I held myself in, telling myself there was time for all of this later, that Jani and I needed to get back home so Grandmother . . . Grandmother . . . Grandmother . . .

Mandalas. I should have made more mandalas. I should never have stopped. In doing so, I had neglected my grandmother; I had neglected her by seeing Richard, by forgetting her health. My grandmother. If only I had made mandalas again, I could have filled a notebook and given them to her. She who loved anything on paper that I did. She who had taught me to draw. My grandmother, my mothering muse. My actions were misguided; I had spent all my excess energy on seeing Richard or mooning over him instead of drawing for her whom I adored.

So on the trip down I began to imagine mandalas, elaborate designs of connections, of cause and effect, of cycles, of the reason for all things, of the reason for my grandmother's death. Why had she been taken from us? What purpose did it serve? What wheel in life was churning that could explain her death? She was still young, not even seventy. We needed her, Jani and I needed her. My mandalas became wheels and trees with mandalas of leaves and mango, mandalas of life. And at the core was my proper grandmother, my bundle of hope.

At first Jani and I sat opposite one another, and turned our heads to look out the window at the same time. We had the compartment to ourselves. We barely spoke to each other, just used head nods and blank expressions. We both had taken baths with strong-smelling soap, as if to present a fresh-faced visage to the world was of utmost importance. We had packed the same way, with care, yet not addressing each other more than necessary. The compartment began to fill up, and two businessmen joined us. At this point, Jani moved over next to me and held my hand.

The power of her grasp. Strength poured out of her hand and surged into mine, so that the energy between us was palpable. Still we refused to look at each other, for any moment our held-in-check world might collapse. I remember reading the *Indian Express* one of the men held. The headlines spoke of the Golden Temple in Amritsar, India. In three months, Indira Gandhi would be dead, and our nations—Sri Lanka, India, Pakistan, and Pi— would be stunned into disbelief. But right now, the fighting was in the background, the world was occupied by other things. So I read a biography of a soccer player in the news, of fans rushing a stadium somewhere in England. All this I read from the back of the businessman's newspaper. Neither he nor his companion said a word, and if they noticed our grief, they were quiet about it. I remember being grateful that they were ordinary-looking businessmen in their suits and ties, with gleaming tiffin-tins at their sides. They helped us keep everything at bay.

We arrived at our station without incident. Great-uncle met us, something we didn't arrange, but didn't question. The only way I can describe our actions then is to say that we danced slowly to a choreographed ballet. Great-uncle had a taxi waiting for us, and we carried our luggage to it. Again, the entire ride was in silence. The cabdriver was kind, infinitely kind as he helped us down at our compound gate. He offered his hand first to Great-uncle, then to Jani, and finally to me. Island cab-drivers as a rule just open doors, and sometimes not even that, since everyone knows opening cab doors is not a great task. But this cabdriver acted as if he were escorting royalty. I think he even forgot about being paid because he was starting to drive off when Jani ran back and paid him through the window.

The family. The funeral. When we climbed up the stairs, my mother stood by the door. Her hair was tied back, her face as well-scrubbed as ours. She was wearing a pale blue sari; it was Jani's, I remember noting.

"Good. You've arrived safely," she said, surveying our luggage.

Jani and I placed our suitcases in the inside hallway and took off our sandals. Everything was quiet. My mother led the three of us inside where a meal awaited us. I remember eating an orange, all the while staring at a mound of rice at the center of the table.

One by one, other relatives began to arrive.

My sisters got there first. Ramani and Savitri, both with round bellies, one clutching the hand of my nephew, Suresh, the other followed by my nieces, Revathi, Usha, and Rukmani. Suddenly the house filled with chatter.

Behind a closed door, my grandmother lay on her side. Not sleeping. My mother began to tell the story.

"She was watering the garden. She was leaning over the marigolds with her hand full of water, a pail in her other hand. I was watching her because I loved to watch her, as you know."

I didn't know.

"She seemed to be admiring the flowers, sprinkling the water, the water catching the light, her hand scooping back for more water. I looked up to see a raven fly overhead. When I looked back at my mother, she was on the ground, the pail overturned, the flowers hidden."

My mother told this story at least a dozen times over the next week, but it was this first telling that I recall with such clarity, that day with my sisters and Jani. My sisters wept at once, scaring their children. Jani took the children to the kitchen to get them milk. My brothers-in-law entered bearing more luggage. My great-uncle went to telephone someone. Soon after that, the house filled with people.

Nineteen

Suddenly, in the absence of noise was noise. There were a great many rites to be performed. Things to do with food and water and smoke and fire. There were mourners to be dealt with, the tide of family and friends who swept through the house in waves. I stayed near the kitchen, suddenly shy. Vasanti gave me small tasks, like shelling peas, picking through the lentils. I helped make the dough for chapatis, while hired cooks, funeral professionals, shaped hundreds of small circles to be cooked.

There were pounds of eggplant, pounds of squash, cabbage and carrots that needed shredding and cutting. Vats of water were boiled to scald potatoes, so their skins would slip off easily. My sisters wandered in and out, commenting on the procession outside, the guests who wanted water and tea. At one point Savitri placed an arm around me and insisted I drink some tea, whereupon I burst into tears.

There was the cremation. And after that, the fuss over whether the remains should be taken to the Ganges near where my grandmother had been born. There was a lot of squabbling and shouting. There were the children getting tired, more people to feed, and lightbulbs to replace (the hallway light chose that time to burn out, giving rise to a tide of commentary over whether that was a good or bad omen). And there was the garden and the marigolds—and oh my grandmother, my grandmother.

I began to make more mandalas. I drew orange, scarlet, and green ones. Colors of Indian independence and then some. I drew spidery webs and chains of dots. But what was the use now that she had died? What was the use when our lives had changed? Three weeks ago everything had been familiar and fine, but now chaos, now an irreversible change in our lives. I could not continue to draw.

Jani found me tossing peas into the garden. We watched as birds came down to feed. "Give your sorrow to the birds. They will fly away with it and sing songs to the Lord," she said. Together we deeply dug out our breath, expanded our chests of mourning, and let our sorrow fly. We did this many, many times. But my sorrow was slow to depart. My sorrow dipped in uneven curves. My sorrow traveled up to the sky and seemed to want to come back to earth again.

My mother found us. With her were my sisters. My mother carried teacups and a teapot on a tray. My sisters carried milk and sugar. We all sat in the garden and drank deeply. We opened a tin of biscuits and dipped them in more tea and ate the soggy result. Never did anything taste so good, the spicy tea and the biscuits. They warmed my tummy and soothed my constricted throat.

My mother bent her head as if to evade her own sorrow. Her face assumed a grave dignity as she gave directions to workmen who came to scale the coconut trees for fruit. Neighbors approached her hesitantly, bringing food, temple offerings. Children from the town stared, to see if they could distinguish her frightful attributes, her witchlike stance. I shooed them away angrily, wanting to protect my mother. She listened to the priests' instructions and fed them.

. . .

Mrs. Narayan came over with an armful of roses. This time I hugged her with all my strength. My mother touched Mrs. Narayan's feet in a gesture of respect. Together we all went to temple. I walked a prathakshana around the shrine for my grandmother and for myself and my mother. I stepped one slow foot against the other, inching my way forward.

I saw my mother in the kitchen kneading and squishing rice that she mixed with yoghurt and buttermilk for my great-uncle's meal. I had never seen her prepare food before, so I stood in the doorway, her figure in profile to me. Then she began to cry, my great mother, my invincible tower of disdain. She was crying into the curd-rice, and wiping her tears with a corner of her sari. Her shoulders shook while she stirred.

All this time I had thought of my grandmother's death as only affecting me, the granddaughter. I had not thought of my mother losing her mother, her own pillar of strength. Of course she and my grandmother had a life full of secrets that predated mine. I was jealous then for my grandmother's attention. If her ghost were watching the two of us, would she bless us both? But there was no ghost. We had cremated my grandmother and sent her to the gods to return to earth again. My sorrow reincarnated as compassion for my mother.

· · ·

I spied on Jani, looked at her slight figure kneeling and praying to Jesus. On her knees for salvation, blessings, help perhaps. Her lips moved in silent prayer. I knew she prayed for us, because Jani told me she did. But what did she pray for herself? Was there nothing she asked for herself?

Perhaps it was three days after the funeral, perhaps more, when my mother received a telegram. Savitri's father, her second husband, was arriving. I knew this because my mother gave me the slip of paper. He offered his sympathy. He was coming by plane, he was landing in Delhi, he was catching the boat to the island. He was arriving soon. When I took the telegram to Savitri, she looked as baffled as I felt, and went on nursing her one-year-old.

One day and one night passed. At noon the next day a taxi arrived in the courtyard and out stepped Ashoka Ram, a middle-aged man with a plump body straining at a brown three-piece Western suit. He had a large yellow handkerchief to wipe his face after he paid the fare. I was on the verandah swing, and he climbed the steps to me.

"Where is Lakshmi?" he asked, bushy eyebrows quivering with impatience.

I didn't know what to say. My mouth went dry, cracking my lips. He was not as I had imagined.

"My mother's inside," I managed.

He went in without another word. I followed to see the commotion.

He spoke to his daughter and admired his grandson. My mother observed him in her witchy way, and was silent. He was brandishing a shining coin in front of the baby. Savitri's face was expressionless. I had never deeply considered my sisters' feelings toward our mother and our various fathers. Maybe they felt as outcast as I did but had immersed themselves in their husbands' lives, and those of their children. Savitri told me that she never thought of our mother, that she had dismissed her from her life, a dead mother.

Meanwhile Ashoka was fumbling with his coin when it suddenly slipped out of his fingers and landed in front of my mother. For an instant everyone froze, then Ashoka was on his hands and knees picking up the coin and touching my mother's feet in obeisance. "Lakshmi," he intoned, this film-land playboy, this phil-anderer, this cad.

My mother turned on her heel and left the room. Ashoka's eyes welled up with tears, as did Savitri's. I too felt weepy and took the baby from my sister. Ashoka and Savitri now confronted one another and fell awkwardly into each other's arms. Opera, opera, opera, went my mind, trying to remain cynical and detached amidst this scene, holding my niece and rocking her body.

Ashoka stayed until the next day. We fixed a cot in the spare room. Ramani and Savitri stayed up most of the night, murmuring, but shooed me away from their whispered conversation. "Marry me," Ashoka asked our mother at least six times, in front of me. My mother said no and watched the cab drive off.

"Why don't you marry him?"

"I don't want to," she replied.

Stupid mother! I couldn't understand her. Marriage could give her respectability, give us respectability, end her sorrow. Marriage could save her.

I watched her with my sisters' children. She wouldn't play with them or hold them. She was a grandmother. But she really wasn't at ease with babies.

Oddly, I began to feel sorry for my mother. As if she guessed my thoughts, she laughed at me, and again I harbored the old familiar hatred.

"You know, Ashoka wasn't always a kind man."

I wasn't surprised.

"We fought bitterly all the time."

"Maybe he has changed," I said.

"He hit me, Sonil. Some things never change."

Twenty

My grandmother used to tell me stories of her childhood. She would speak of the Tamil New Year, Holi, the Harvest Festival, the Festival of Lights, harbingers of the seasons. She spoke of her own mother getting up early to bathe in the river, sweeping away all the past unhappy days in one immersion, and rising refreshed, ready to face a new season. Dry season, wet season, those were our seasons, hot and less hot. But if one watched closely enough, one could discern a spring and summer, a fall and winter. There were minute changes, a shift in the air, a different kind of blooming bud.

Changes brought illness. A shift in the wind, and I'd come down with a cold and cough. The monsoons brought mosquitoes, which brought malaria. Perhaps grief brought about my laryngitis, it is hard to say. In any case, I found myself ill and in bed.

. . .

Jani brought rice with petite peas and tiny spiced potatoes to my room. My mother came too, and together we
ate dahl spooned over the rice. Jani and my mother drew
chairs up near my bed, and I sat up to eat my meal. No
one spoke much. Jani was still wary of my mother, I noticed. I still distrusted my mother, despite her disclosure
about Ashoka. Grief allowed me to feel pity for her, but
my heart was more cautious. I ate without tasting.

Elephants mourn their dead with copious tears and a
thrashing of tree branches. When an elephant herd
comes across the bones of a departed member, it caresses
what's left and grieves the loss. Baby calves will not part
from their dead mother's body for a long time, and if one
observes closely, one can discern the haunted look in
their eyes as they wait for her to come back to life. My
mother wore such a look, dark rings around her eyes, her
nose red with crying.

But here she was speaking of her own childhood, her
life with my grandmother.

"She would wake us at four sometimes to listen to
the hum of insects and birds awakening. Other times,
if the next day was a festival, she let us stay up late and
help the cook prepare the food. We'd cook while it was
dark outside. She insisted we girls learn to cook and
mend and manage money, for she wanted us to become

fair, good wives. But she never counted on Shalani and Leila marrying foreigners. Partly to please her, I married Balu, a man who was old enough to be my father. We lived at his mother's house in Kerala. He was a strict man, insistent on order—the socks had to be rolled just so, the books stacked alphabetically—and he was thrifty. He would daily measure out how many grams of dahl I could use, how much ghee. His mother naturally thought I was conjuse—miserly—in my cooking. We are not poor, she'd say, and I could not tell her it was her son's hand that made the bread dry. He never touched me after our wedding night."

Why was she telling me this? Did I need to know such details? And what was Jani thinking of it all?

"After he died, I met Ashoka. I was paid attention to for the first time. He promised me roses and champagne and Bombay. I didn't know that he promised these things to all his girls, and that there were many girls. Even the night before we ran off to Bombay, he paid his mistress a visit that took hours more than a simple goodbye. He told me his women were crazy, that his mistress here wanted to kill herself, that his mistress there had a disease. He swore to be faithful in the north. After Savitri was born, I stopped listening to him.

"I met your father much later. I didn't even like him at first. We met at the library, and later he came to a reading by my friend the poet. We had dinner that night, and listening to him, I saw that here was a man who knew what he wanted to do with his life. He had a passion, which Ashoka never did. He was devoted to his photography. Our courtship was slow—I know what people say, that we leapt into bed immediately, but that's not true. Ashoka had flattered me with his attention but your father took me seriously. I fell in love as I never had before."

I longed to speak but my throat ached. Her forwardness was startling, but my mother was never one to do what was expected. Perhaps my grandmother's death released her history.

"But I must have been born between two warring planets. After six months, your father told me he had been married once before, and had two children. He and his wife had separated and he didn't get custody. I was not as shocked as you might suppose, for hadn't I a past as well, and children besides? We planned a life together—we would buy a house, up north on the island, plant a garden. I dreamed of rows of roses and climbing jasmine. I envisioned blue daisies and canahambra.

"Of course it was never to be. He received a letter. His wife had been killed in an accident. His daughter was a heroin addict, his son a thief." She gave a short laugh. "I told him he had to go and help them. He begged me to come with him, but I felt that he needed to go alone, that it wasn't right for his children to see me just yet. We parted in March.

"Who can say what happened? He didn't write. Did

America change him? Certainly I must have occupied a smaller and smaller place in his heart. Maybe he met with an accident. I was pregnant with you, and he didn't know. Madame Butterfly on Pi. It was like a bad Tamil film."

Her voice turned comic, her own solution to unhappiness. My throat ached with something more than sickness. Jani had tears in her eyes. My cowboy dad had ridden into the sunset, vanished without a trace, leapt on his horse and kept on riding. Exit the hero.

I thought of those monks who swept their sand mandalas into the river. Beauty, perfection, all so momentary. Circled perfection was not a constant in their lives—a life centered on God, bowls of food, occasional television. Other artists carve in stone, try to make their work immortal. But the Taj gets polluted, the Sphinx gets worn away, the jewels are knocked out of the idol's eyes. The monks knew that nothing was permanent and kicked their creation to oblivion at once. They didn't fool themselves. My parents had had an illusion of happiness, my mother had dreamed of a garden. They had held hands and planned. If they had known better, they would have parted as soon as they met. They wouldn't have tried to mock the gods with their unconventional coupling.

But like ants who keep working no matter what, we try to control our own lives, tunnel paths to ideals and wants, unaware that an accidental footstep will knock everything asunder. I was old enough to get by on instinct, I thought. But listening to my mother changed my life. I think it was that night that I learned not to take anything for granted, that no future was ever secure. But what was there to hold on to? What gave us hope?

"I want to go to college in America. I want to meet my father," I told her, not because I felt I had to, but because it was the only thing I could say with my hoarse throat.

"Look," she said as if she hadn't heard, "life is not easy. You need more than good looks and good marks to get you by in this world. And it's not merely intelligence, either. It's practicality that is at issue. Do you have what it takes to live away from this island, from India itself? Can you maintain yourself beyond your imagination?"

I listened, not wanting to listen. Maybe I listened with the part of myself that wasn't immediately equipped to listen, like the way dolphins can listen without having ears. I listened with that part of myself that would hear what she said years later.

But she went on: "I am not the only one of this opinion. Your father would agree with me. Freedom does not come easily in this world. It is not about having a perfect dress, or a perfect view, or even a paradise of a room. It is not about going to college on another continent, or even finding your father. It is about how you can survive after things are taken from you. It is about the prospect of losing what you love and the effort it takes to continue.

"Life is not romantic. Romance is hard to come by.

Romance does not always work," said my mother, looking away.

Imagine the scene. My mother in a dark green sari, bold lipstick, her arms full of poetry. My father in dusty jeans—jeans splattered with darkroom chemicals—reaching for a book on still-life painting. Perhaps with her head in the clouds she ran into him—literally—and her books scattered at her feet. And he bent down to retrieve them and glanced up to find the single most beautiful face looking at him. His hair bristled. Her eyes turned to stars. But this was not youthful infatuation, so they dismissed their instincts and apologized and parted.

Later, the poet read of women making love with their mouths and silken skin and strong desire. As the poet read, my mother's eyes wandered, and seeing him, she blushed. *I touch your neck and watch it flame and then I let my hand slide over your breast.* He couldn't stop looking at her. *I undo the buttons slowly and your breath is alive with longing.* They smiled and shifted in their seats. *I tongue your heart and plunge lower.* They felt a pulse in their inner parts.

At tea, they said hello shyly and felt self-conscious. In three hours, when they are seated at a riverbank, he will lean toward her and recite the poet's lines, and she will be astonished. Unconsciously she will unbutton her blouse.

They will circle each other and tell each other they

are too old for foolishness. They will pretend indifference. But one day he would unfold the pleats in her sari
and she would reveal herself like a forgotten package.
The earth would sigh with their pleasure and later their
love. I would not be thought of, but there would be other
ideas.

My mother would dream of planting in the spring,
using terracotta pots. She will think of harvesting herbs
and edible flowers, mulching trees bearing orange and
lemon, watering beds. Her own bed would be damp,
mussed, never completely made. She sketched the plants
she might use, feeling tingles from the night still. He
might steal behind her and wrap her in his arms. My
Indian rose, my Eastern star. They would have a house
and later a family.

The letter was airmail blue, thin. Typeface from a
lawyer with a note from a concerned aunt. How had it
been forwarded? Through the institution that funded his
year in India. Her decision had been swift, resolute. He
must act the hero, the knight, the savior. He must save
his children as she could not save hers. They had all the
time in the world, after all.

Had there been a train crash? Did his head get hurt
and did he suffer amnesia? Did he fight with his daughter to go to rehab, threaten his son with jail? Did they
enter his room one night and pour hot poison in his ear?
Did a meddlesome relative bar his passage back? Did no
one know?

Or had he simply succumbed to life in the West, traded his jeans for an Armani suit, paid his bills, let his photography languish, come to his senses? Had he known that there were no real love stories in the world and that to contemplate happiness was to invite pain? Did he seal his heart and airbrush her from his life?

Who was the cruelest of my mother's lovers?

Twenty-one

My family was something precious, like jewelry, like a necklace you never take off. My family was deep as a rose, true as any tree. As my mother spoke to me that day, my laryngitis abated, and I felt that I knew something, just as I had always yearned. But I was so shocked and overcome with all that had happened to me, I began to yawn, and my throat began to hurt a little, and I began to think of cold fruit juice or ice cream and merely smiled at my mother to thank her. She let me rest. I recovered rapidly.

After all the ceremonies were over, after all the guests had left, when the house was once again empty and we were four, not five, but just four, we began to make plans.

When my grandmother died, my great-uncle played

the veena for nine days in a row. He had been devoted to her. She had once convinced my grandfather to open a gallery for him. My grandfather planned while my great-uncle painted. For days, they were confident of success. But my great-uncle felt the lure of opium once too often, and my grandfather fought with him. My grandfather vowed never to have anything to do with him again. My grandmother pleaded his cause but to no avail. My great-uncle left town to study with a veena master. My grandfather died on a mountain when I was three years old. My great-uncle returned for his funeral and stayed. He would remain now, as would my mother.

Jani was returning to the convent. "I'm not saying I'll never get married, but I want to go, to finish what I started. I've found a kind of peace there that I haven't had since Asha died," she said.

"How long has she been—since she died?"

"Four months ago. Her mother wrote me. She had lymph cancer that was detected too late. All winter she thought she just had a cold and never bothered to see a doctor. . . . So I want to go back to the nuns."

"What about studies?"

"I'll manage without. Maybe I'll join you in your America and finish there. I won't stay away too long," she promised me. I felt she was teasing me, pretending that America was as easy to get to as Bombay.

We spoke of Grandmother. To my surprise, I learned that Jani felt responsible for her demise, in a small way.

"If only I had stayed at home and agreed to marriage, she could have gone in peace. I worried her needlessly. I gave her much cause for pain." She paused. "Going to the convent was perhaps a mistake then. To go there now seems infinitely correct."

"I could have paid more attention to Grandmother, not been so distracted," I said.

"You are too young, and anyway that American took advantage of you."

"No, he didn't, Jani. I liked him too much, beyond reason."

"Reason seems to be rarely involved in love."

Jani began to pack.

"I still want to examine this cloistered life. We all of us live in cloisters," said Jani before tossing her cashmere shawl into her bag.

"Hey, how come you are taking pretty clothes to the convent? Jani, what's going on?"

She laughed and said airily, "I don't have a secret life, Sonil. I'm taking my shawl because the nights are sometimes cold."

I would go back to Madras. My mother and my great-uncle would manage in the house, with Vasanti to help and Kirti, as well. My mother would take care of the garden; my great-uncle would take less opium.

Twenty-two

A few weeks later Richard returned. He rang me up, and my mother wordlessly handed me the receiver. He said he and Maria were having lunch together, and asked if I wanted to join them.

I biked over to the restaurant they had chosen. I wasn't sure what it would be like seeing him, and my heart was skipping like a jump rope. I told myself it didn't matter at all; I had already said goodbye. Still, when I saw him, I ran into his arms and hugged him. He was tanner, but seemed shorter. Maria looked the same as ever. We sat down to a Sri Lankan meal of milk rice and curried vegetables, everything appealing and tasty and in small portions. I told them about Grandmother, and Maria hugged me. Richard spoke of Ethiopia. He'd had a hard time until his mother abandoned

Helen Koenig and joined him at a cooperative farm. Together, they worked with Red Cross volunteers. Richard was going back to Ethiopia; his mother was returning to New York, spiritually content.

I spoke of Radcliffe; I spoke of zoology. I spoke until I got bored and longed to go home.

Love is funny. Every man I have loved since Richard has been a kind of protest, a defiant gesture against loneliness and isolation. Was I merely that kind of distraction for him, some way to buy time? I can't make up my mind. Ten years after he left me, he married a girl from Kerala and now has three children. We don't keep in touch. Once he was in the same city as me and telephoned. He had gotten my number from Maria, still on Pi. His voice was like an evocation of the past, but I didn't want to see him. I had erased him from my life in the manner I suppose my mother had erased my father. I had ceased to remember how he smelled or how my head fit on his shoulder. I had stopped lighting the candle that kept his presence alive; the altar was cold.

But for years I saw his face in the faces of strangers on the street. He had imprinted me, and I was attracted to men like him for a long time. Once, I had read, there was a whooping crane that had been brought up in captivity. When it was time for her to breed, she rejected all the male cranes who came to call on her. Instead, she flirted with the man who had fed her from birth. In the name of science, this man courted her, hunted earthworms for her, and danced for her, as well, to ready her mating phase. Duly, she was artificially inseminated, but she believed the father to be a six-foot man in jeans.

Hearts have no sense; we love what we love.

About the time of Richard's marriage, Jani wrote to me. She had met the mad preacher and consented to give birth to his child. She hadn't given up women, but somehow his skewed religion appealed to her, and she became involved. If she found him sexy, I never knew. The baby wasn't Jesus, of course, but then perhaps all babies are born in the image of God. Perhaps the spirit of the Divine inhabits every child. Certainly that is what our family thought, giving children allowance to help themselves to offerings meant for the gods. Go to an Indian concert, and you will see children running amok in the aisles, climbing onto the stage, the parents not minding. Children were innocent, sacred and privileged. Jani had the baby, and they named him Dove, which means peace bird, or "where is" in Italian, and "a smoky dark color," as well. The preacher lives with Jani, but has his own lover, as does Jani. I think they are happier than most. I think of them passing quiet evenings together—quiet since both were not given to talking. Perhaps he stopped smoking ganja, perhaps he had cut his hair and was less mad. I could imagine the two of them putting on a Dylan album and dancing with their child.

I have not yet found my true love, and sometimes doubt that I will. I can imagine living in a cabin in the wilderness with two large dogs for companions. I do not long to share my life with someone else anymore. Love has failed so many people I know. The poet writes of this often. She says love is like a golden blossom that sprouts at the footfall of Buddha, sprung from pure joy and adoration. But the beloved walks away without a glance. It seems the moment we meet someone, we are preparing to depart from him, just as our every breath brings us closer to death.

Should I never have loved? Should I have saved my heart? Maybe, yet what good would it have done me? I might never have known the rapture of sadness, as the poet says, the heights of despair, the ecstasy of agony. You can never escape one for the other. But I am not a philosopher, and I cannot make rules for the way to live my life. I am not that strong. Every time I swear never to fall in love again, my head is turned by the sight of a pretty face. My heart again fills with song, readying for heartbreak. Often I spend more time in recovery from love lost than in love itself. It is distraction and selfishness, but sometimes it is all I have.

After I left the island, I threw myself into my studies. Taking exams always terrified me. I would arrive very early and sit in an exam hall while the proctors walked through the aisles, grimly handing out exam booklets. Soon, all would be quiet, except for the shuffling sound of feet skimming the floor in rhythmic agitation and the ticking of the clock. As always, I would lose myself in the test questions, busy with my pen, writing an essay.

My pre-college teachers believed in long, complex questions that required long and complex answers. Three hours would fly past as we addressed ourselves to history or science, reimagining experiments carried out in labs, the combinations of chemicals. Sometimes the answer was in the question itself, and sometimes the answer would only present itself in the writing.

I also read at home and went to the movies with my aunts and cousins. I even began to play cricket, since one of my younger cousins wanted to practice. I learned to swing my bat with a minimum of effort and learned to bowl properly.

My mother visited me every several weeks. It seemed to do her good to get off the island and see Madras. There were still many things unspoken between us, but I was learning that she was a complex person, and oddly shy as well. The effort of raising her daughters had been too great for her, so she gave us away to those who could. She tried to repair the damage she had done by listening to my sisters and downplaying her extravagance with perfume and such. She treated us to tea at the Taj Hotel and got idlis from Woodlands in the mornings. Sometimes she and I would walk on the beach, not talking, but comfortable.

Eventually, I did pass the big qualifying exam and went on to gain admission at Radcliffe. It was colder than I expected, and there were so many things to learn at once, but I bundled up and settled in after the first year. I studied hard, wanting to justify my voyage overseas. When I felt I could not study anymore, I thought of my grandmother and how proud she might be of my achievements. I declared zoology as my major.

I joined an Indian Association and even went to the Indian temple on occasion. At first I spent all my time studying, but then I fell in with a group of international students. We spent Sunday afternoons making fun of the MIT engineers and drinking cappuccinos and reading fashion magazines. I found I could be as shallow as the best of them. My taste for rock and roll grew, but nostalgia for the father I had mythologized made me listen to country music as well. One night after dancing too much, I stumbled into a tattoo parlor—it was just a room in someone's house—and got a small OM needled onto my ankle.

I traveled cross-country in a Ford Escort with some friends and looked up my father. He lived in Missouri, somewhere on the outskirts of Kansas City. I spent a weekend calling up all the Donaldsons in the state after

I wormed his name and residence from my mother. She was appalled that I wanted to call him, but I told her that she owed me. I didn't tell her, of course, that I was going to try to visit.

He wasn't a cowboy, but he had on a plaid shirt that first day. He also had a big black Labrador named Shirley, and together we took her for a walk. My father was still a photographer and worked long hours in the darkroom. He hadn't married but was not that interested in hearing about my mother.

I told him a little about myself. I guess I liked him, but he was hard to fathom. I looked at his photographs and some caught my eye. One entitled "Goan Spring" pictured a young girl, head thrown back and laughing, holding a sprig of fresh, bright green peanuts, her smile wide, and I liked her instantly. Another featured a round man, also from India, talking animatedly to a patron in his shop. In the background was a light-bearded man who reminded me of Richard. I asked my father the date of the photograph.

"Nineteen eighty-four," he replied.

"Eighty-four?"

"Yes . . . spring, I think," he said, busy with his chemical processing.

"You were in India so recently?"

"Yes . . . what . . . oh. Yeah, I guess you were there. Well. I couldn't really visit. Your mother made that very clear, early on."

"What do you mean?"

"After I left your mother, it took a year for me to put everything in order. My daughter never really quit drugs, but she did enter a program. My son resented me and considered me the cause of everything wrong in his and his sister's lives. I offered to help, to let him move in with me, to pay for college. He joined the army and never wrote. I missed your mother but never wrote. I couldn't. I wanted to fix things and return to her. Maybe I wasn't ready to give myself absolutely to her and wanted to see if I could make it alone. But all I could do was think of her. So I decided my children weren't being helped by my presence and that I had a right to love. But your mother disagreed. She felt I couldn't abandon my children."

"My mother said that?"

"Something to that effect."

"What happened?"

"Nothing. I begged her to come to the States, to bring your sisters, but she refused. She never told me there was another child. I heard about you years later, through a mutual friend. By then, I let things be. It seemed senseless to try and patch things up."

By this time, I was learning to ride over whatever astonishing disclosures my family habitually provided for me. How could she deny him in her life? Perhaps the same way she had denied me. I guess she had been wounded, but weren't we all wounded?

"You know," he said, "she was always the subject of

gossip. You might have heard some . . . out-of-proportion stories. She's an independent woman, fearless, and it makes people suspicious. I think people like to think she's wanton, having enormous appetites." He smiled. "She is not as people might say."

"I think she had a lot of . . . male friends," I said.

"She attracts men. She likes to take long walks by herself. Her absences probably give rise to rumor."

I didn't want to say that I had believed them, too. I continued to look at more pictures. He was talented, my father, but not famous. Perhaps he still loved my mother in the way I loved Richard, maybe even more. I had to stop trying to figure them out; they were changeable and in motion. I had thought for so long that they defined me, that I would be a repetition of them. I had thought that inheritance was inescapable. It is, but not in the ways I had imagined. My family is ingrained in my actions; they are uppermost in my mind. Yet there are parts of me that are nothing like them; I am a random mix of genes and attributes. I do not have to be like my mother. I am not destined to walk in her shadow. Yet a shard of her exists in everything I do, in the way I look at men, in the way I view my life. My grandmother is in my heart, a mandala I never part with, and my mother is the necklace I never take off. My father, my father is a hat, protecting me from sun and rain, but a hat I can lift off at will.

I returned to the photographs. There were some

from Sri Lanka, from Tibet and Nepal. A few from Indonesia, Pakistan, Japan, and China. Several from Alaska. In an album, I came across his American series and there were the prairies I had dreamed about, gently tinted in a violet wash. Here was a California coast, a slice of Chicago, a meditation on a lake in Minnesota. And there was Boston, my new home, taken in winter, snow clinging to the steps, beckoning me back.

ACKNOWLEDGMENTS

This small book was long in writing and many people
helped me along the way. I would like to thank my dear
friends for their support and encouragement; my teachers Mr. William Gifford and Ms. Brett Singer for their
wisdom early on; Bonnie, Theresa, and Julia for help in
preparing the manuscript; Bob Cornfield, Max Eilen-
berg, and Dan Franklin for years of patience; Anica
Alvarez, Ann Close, and Nelly Bly for their faith and ex-
pertise; Sandra Dijkstra for her understanding and
relentless prodding; my parents for their steadfastness;
my brother Shridar for his humor; and my students for
often forgiving a distracted teacher.

A NOTE ON THE TYPE

The text of this book was set in Centaur, the only typeface designed by Bruce Rogers, the well-known American book designer. A celebrated penman, Rogers based his design on the roman face cut by Nicolas Jenson in 1470 for his Eusebius. Jenson's roman surpassed all of its forerunners and even today, in modern recuttings, is one of the most popular and attractive of all typefaces.

The italic used to accompany Centaur is Arrighi, designed by Frederic Warde, also an American, and based on a Chancery face used by Ludovico degli Arrighi in 1524.

Composed, printed, and bound by R. R. Donnelley & Sons, Harrisonburg, Virginia

Designed by Dorothy Schmiderer Baker